Is Daisy losing the man she loves?

Daisy watched Jack out of the corner of her eye and couldn't help smiling at the way he was getting into the music—grinning, tapping his foot, clapping to the beat.

When the girls were finished, he was the first to call out, "Encore. Encore."

"How about 'Short'nin' Bread,' girls. That's one of your best," Rebecca suggested.

Daisy followed Jack's gaze as he turned toward Rebecca, and she saw his expression alter. So subtly that had she not known him so well. . .loved him so much. . .she would never have discerned it.

The look was deeper than regard. His heart was in his eyes.

Daisy's was suddenly in her throat.

She turned away.

A painful realization began to seep into her spirit.

RACHEL DRUTEN is a native Californian. She is an artist as well as an author, wife, mother, and grandmother. Much of her time is devoted to overseeing a non-profit, on-site, after-school program in the arts for disadvantaged children, kindergarten through fifth grade.

Books by Rachel Druten

HEARTSONG PRESENTS
HP312—Out of the Darkness (with Dianna Crawford)
HP363—Rebellious Heart
HP508—The Dark Side of the Sun
HP551—Healing Heart

He Loves Me,
He Loves Me Not

Rachel Druten

Heartsong Presents

This book is dedicated to my daughter, Noël, and all my nieces, whose selfless efforts as mothers, wives and independent women reflect the strengths that set Daisy apart: (listed alphabetically) Karen, Mahvash and "little" Rachel; but especially "little" Tanja, the inspiration for Daisy, whose breathless joy hides a strength that can move mountains—and has.

And, as always, this book is dedicated to my 93 year-old mother, Noël Bryant "Oma," who has kept us all together.

To my dedicated and loving "critiquers," mentor Dianna Crawford, Sheila Herron, and Barbara Wilder; and my husband Charles with his red pencil. To Tracie Peterson for her understanding, support and patience, and all the others at Barbour Publishing with whom I am proud to be associated.

A note from the Author:
I love to hear from my readers! You may correspond with me by writing:

Rachel Druten
Author Relations
PO Box 719
Uhrichsville, OH 44683

ISBN 1-59310-431-6

HE LOVES ME, HE LOVES ME NOT

Our mission is to publish and distribute inspirational products offering exceptional value and biblical encouragement to the masses.

All scripture quotations are taken from the King James Version of the Bible.

All of the characters and events in this book are fictitious. Any resemblance to actual persons, living or dead, or to actual events is purely coincidental.

PRINTED IN THE U.S.A.

Or check out our Web site at www.heartsongpresents.com

one

Summer 1948

"Don't be so condescending, Jack McCutcheon. Remember, I knew you before you affixed *Reverend* to your name." Daisy Fielding tossed her hair back and glared at him.

A willowy waitress paused at their table. "More coffee?" She smiled at the handsome, sandy-haired minister, ignoring Daisy who was sitting across from him in a corner booth at Feingold's Deli.

"Yes, please," Daisy snapped.

The server's gaze still on Jack, she topped off Daisy's cup, until coffee spilled over into the saucer.

"Thank you." Jack flashed Daisy a grin and turned his most charming smile on the pretty, dark-haired waitress as she carefully filled his cup.

When she had gone, Daisy muttered, "Don't be so smug, Jack. It's your *uniform*. Some women just can't resist trying to corrupt a cleric."

Jack threw back his head and laughed. Daisy hadn't heard him laugh like that in a long while: white teeth flashing, brown eyes slits of mirth. It sent a little tingle of pleasure through her, even though she was still plenty irritated with him.

He took a swallow of coffee. "So, what were we talking about?"

"You were belittling my reading material." She glanced at the copy of *Mademoiselle* lying beside her on the red Naugahyde seat.

"You're too sensitive, Daisy. Just because I tease you about the profundity"—he grinned—"or lack thereof, of the women's magazines you devour, you take it as demeaning your intellect."

"It's not what you say, Jack, it's how you say it. And the expression on your face." Glaring at him, she lifted her cup, sloshing coffee onto her canary yellow cashmere sweater. "Oh, Jack. Look what you made me do." She smacked the cup back down into its saucer.

"I'm not demeaning your intelligence, Daisy, or belittling you. I'm just suggesting you might consider broadening your interests."

Daisy dipped the corner of her napkin in her water glass and began dabbing at the stains on her sweater. "To include more Bible reading I suppose."

Jack frowned. "You're missing the point. It's not just about what you read. To put it bluntly, Daisy, you need to do something constructive with your life. You need balance."

"What would you know about my life, Jack? We've hardly seen each other since Court and Rebecca's wedding. Besides, I do have balance. I'm second vice president of the Spinsters, and I'm on the hospitality committee at the club, which takes a lot more time than you'd think. And during the war—not all that long ago—I rolled bandages for the Red Cross Tuesday and Thursday afternoons, and I volunteered almost full time at the Hollywood Canteen entertaining our soldiers."

"That is all very commendable. And I haven't forgotten how you took care of Court after he was wounded. But the war's over, Court's a hundred percent, and"— Jack paused—"and he has a wife to take care of him."

The pensive look that slid across his face did not go unnoticed by Daisy. In fact, there wasn't much about Jack McCutcheon she didn't notice.

She'd seen that sad, distracted expression more than once lately. Oh, he still had the abundant charm and the charismatic fervor of his faith. But somewhere, somehow, that spark of spirit that had made their relationship so cherished and special to her had dimmed. She was determined to find out why.

Jack cleared his throat, glanced down at the table knife he was toying with, and looked up. "All I'm suggesting is that you're too talented and smart to spend your days consuming fashion magazines, playing bridge, and shopping for a new outfit to wear to the next country club dance."

Daisy slapped her napkin on the table. "That clerical collar has squeezed all the fun out of you, Jack. You used to be good company. Now you sound like a stuffed shirt." Her eyes narrowed. "And more like my brother every day. Did Court put you up to this?"

Jack didn't answer.

"I knew it. Court thinks I should get a job." She picked up her napkin and wiped her lips. "I say, when I spend my money I'm providing jobs for other people."

"I applaud your altruism." Jack gave her a benign look. "In that case, have you ever thought of volunteering some of your time to charity?"

Is the man deaf? Daisy gathered up her purse and magazine. "I already do. I'm also helping with makeup for the Headdress Ball, and I answer the phone in the Junior League office one morning a week—don't roll your eyes, Jack." She scooted out of the booth. "I get enough lectures from Court. I don't need them from you."

As she flounced toward the door, Jack murmured, "And you might start attending church more often, too."

Daisy stopped abruptly and spun around. "Why should I bother to go to church? I can get my own private sermons from you right here."

For a moment, she observed him in silence. Then a shut-him-up thought sprang forth. "I have a volunteer idea. How about if I lead the Bible study class for the high school girls? You said you needed somebody to do it."

"You?" Jack did not hide his amusement.

Daisy lifted her chin. "I'll bet I'm almost as knowledgeable about the Bible as you are. I took courses in college, you know."

"Because they were required."

"So? I got an A. Ask me a question! Go ahead."

Jack frowned. "Don't be ridiculous, Daisy. This isn't a competition."

"How many girls are in the high school class?"

"Maybe five or six. . .when they all show up."

Daisy scoffed. "Five or six? Even I can handle five or six. In fact, I'll bet I can quadruple that number in a month— Oh, I forgot, gambling is against your religion."

"And yours," Jack said.

"Not if it's for a dinner. Would you wager a home-cooked meal?"

"Have you ever tasted my cooking?" Jack made a face. "I lose my appetite thinking about it."

"So, already you're prepared to lose. In that case," Daisy said as she tossed her magazine onto the table, "*Mademoiselle* has a great food section. Maybe it'll give you some ideas."

Jack slid out of the booth. At six feet four inches tall and broad-shouldered, he loomed over Daisy. He reached for the check. . .and the magazine. "What's the duration of this wager?"

"Give me two months," Daisy said, turning on her heel, "and you'll witness wonders." Over her shoulder, she said, "Speaking of food—for your information, I just finished reading Steinbeck's *The Grapes of Wrath*. Maybe we can discuss that instead of me the next time we meet for coffee."

two

Good Shepherd Community Church was located at the corner of Third Street and York Boulevard on the border of blue-collar and middle-class neighborhoods.

In his office overlooking the center patio, Jack glanced at the clock on his desk. It was 3:45. No Daisy. And class was supposed to start in ten minutes.

Just like her to be late—or forget. *She's as ditzy now as when she was a kid*, he thought, inclined to be less charitable toward her than usual.

The church secretary's voice crackled through the intercom. "There's a call for you on line one. It's Courtney Fielding."

"Thanks, Mrs. Beemer." Jack picked up the phone. "Hi, Court. I'd hoped it was your sister."

"Why Daisy?"

"She volunteered to teach the girls' Bible study class."

"She what?" Court snorted. "What qualifies Daisy for that job?"

"To hear her tell it, plenty. It was a wager, of sorts. But that's another story. Anyway, she's not here."

"Probably getting her nails done."

"Wouldn't surprise me." Jack sighed. "I guess I'll have to get Mrs. Beemer to fill in. I've got a couple of shut-ins that are expecting me, or I'd take the class myself.

So. . .what's up with you and Rebecca?"

"My wife's in the mood to fuss," Court said. "For dinner she's making roast beef with Yorkshire pudding and all the trimmings. We thought if you were free—"

"What time?" As a bachelor, he tried not to miss a home-cooked meal. Especially one prepared by Rebecca.

"Six thirty?"

"I'll be there."

"Good luck with Daisy," Court said, and the line went dead.

"I'll need it." Jack dropped the receiver into its cradle, scooted his chair back from the desk, and stood up.

Despite their diverse backgrounds, Jack's blue-collar, Court's decidedly upper-crust, he and Court had been closer than brothers since boyhood. Jack was grateful they still were.

Not long ago, though, their friendship had been sorely tested. From the moment he'd set eyes on the woman who was now Court's wife, Jack had been deeply attracted to her. He remembered her standing on the church steps the day after she'd first arrived in California. Tall and beautiful with a vulnerability and goodness shining in her large brown eyes. . .and brave. A young war widow crossing the Pacific with her four-year-old boy to work as a housekeeper in the home of strangers. She'd proved as fine as she was lovely, and even more patient as she put up with Court's dark days of rehabilitation from the war.

Absently, Jack reached for his jacket draped over the back of the desk chair.

Jack had fallen in love with her.

She'd fallen in love with Court.

It was a blow as deep as death. Or so it had seemed at the time.

Ministers weren't supposed to have the feelings of jealousy and anger that had overwhelmed him. Ministers were above base, human impulses. Ministers were pure in spirit. Or so went the rumor.

He'd discovered the dark side of himself in those days.

He slipped into his jacket.

As a young preacher the Lord's words had come easily, almost glibly, to his lips. He'd been confident and charismatic in the pulpit. Prideful of the talents with which God had gifted him.

But He who sees all had seen Jack's pride—and dealt with it.

It had been a battle. But God had finally won. As a result, Jack's faith had deepened, his commitment restored. From then on he knew he had been able to counsel and preach from a more understanding heart.

Even though he no longer coveted his best friend's wife, from time to time he still wondered if he would ever find another woman like Rebecca.

At that moment the door flung open.

He glanced at the clock and sighed deeply. *Speaking of opposites...*

Daisy limped into his office. Her blond curls were scrambled. A strand of pink ribbon hung over one eye. Dirt splashed her ruffled white blouse and down the front of her flared pink-and-white checked skirt. Her hose were ripped, and her white sandals were gray with grime.

"Would you believe a car ran over my Bible?" she wailed, dropping into the leather chair in front of Jack's desk. "It's a sacrilege."

She looked about to cry.

Jack put his hand on the arm of the chair and knelt in front of her. "Daisy, what happened to you?"

"I tripped over the curb." She was clutching an oversized white patent leather handbag and a limp-looking Bible with a broken binding, a chevron of dirty tire marks across its face. "My car died at the corner of York and Colorado."

"That's at least a mile and a half from here."

"Don't I know it."

Gently he examined her skinned knee—as he'd done off and on since she was eight years old. "A little hydrogen peroxide ought to take care of it." He looked up. "Do you hurt anyplace else?"

"Only my pride." She glared at him. "I knew if I didn't get here on time you'd think I'd forgotten."

Jack felt a twinge of guilt. "Better that than breaking a leg. What about your car?"

"Some nice man pushed it to the curb. Don't worry, it's not going anyplace. I can have it picked up after class."

Jack stood up. "You don't look in any condition to handle the class. I'll get Mrs. Beemer to fill in for you."

"That proves it!" Daisy stood up and pushed him aside. "I knew you didn't trust me."

"Don't be so sensitive, Daisy. I know you always have the best intentions."

"Don't try to placate me, Jack," she said, limping toward the door. "I've known you long enough not to be fooled by your silver-tongued rhetoric. You didn't really expect I would follow through on my commitment. Well, regardless, you're not going to get out of our wager that easily."

"I'm not trying to—"

"I'm going to the ladies' room to clean up." She turned. "Please be so kind as to tell the girls I will be there shortly."

three

In the ladies' room, Daisy tucked her ruffled blouse into her wide, patent leather belt and attacked the smudges on her skirt with a wet towel.

Not perfect, but it would have to do.

She then fished around in her oversized handbag and pulled out a lipstick, a jeweled powder case, rouge, and a comb, all of which she lined up on the counter in front of her.

Glaring back at her reflection in the mirror over the sink, she yanked the comb through her tangle of curls so hard her eyes watered.

Teaching a Bible study class, of all things. It was degrading the lengths she was willing to go to get the man's attention. And for what? Obviously Jack still only saw her as Court's bothersome little sister. When all she wanted was for him to see her as a woman.

She squinted into the mirror, reapplied her makeup, then dropped the cosmetics back into her purse and snapped it closed.

Well, too late now. She was stuck with this silly wager, and there was no way, *no way* that she wouldn't pull it off. Even if Jack never did appreciate her or see her as a woman.

She did have her pride, after all.

Picking up her handbag and her Bible, she limped out of the restroom and down the hall.

Outside the classroom she paused, listening to the muffled, disgruntled voices within. Taking a deep breath, she pushed open the door.

The room fell silent. Four sets of curious eyes targeted her entrance with the critical assessment possessed only by teenage girls.

The small room was rectangular, just large enough to accommodate the pine library table in the center. Ten chairs were pulled up to it, four of them occupied.

Three of the girls returned tentative smiles, the fourth, at the far end of the table, resumed painting her fingernails.

"Sorry I'm late. My car broke down," Daisy explained, sliding into the nearest chair.

The fingernail painter glanced at a thin-banded watch on her wrist. "This class is supposed to end at five o'clock. I'm out of here in a half hour."

"I'll make sure we all are," Daisy replied benignly, inwardly appalled at the girl's audacity.

No point in making a point at this juncture.

"I'm Daisy Fielding." She set down her purse, Bible, and the folder Jack had given her and took a moment to scan the upturned faces, a motley mix of teenage acne.

If only they knew there are products out there that could help them.

"At least we have time to get acquainted," Daisy said, pulling an attendance sheet from the folder. "Raise your hand when I call your name, and maybe you can say a few words about what you expect from the class."

"For one thing, we expected it to be coed," muttered the nail polisher, whose name turned out to be Meredith.

She was a large-boned girl with bobbed black hair and a slash of bangs above dark eyebrows that had yet to see a pair of tweezers.

"We kind of expected that Pastor Jack would be our teacher," added Rita, a scrawny young thing with a frizz of red hair. She pushed her horn-rimmed glasses back up her freckled nose. "No offense."

"None taken."

What red-blooded teenage girl wouldn't hope to get her young, handsome, single, ex-marine minister for a Bible study teacher? For that matter, what red-blooded twenty-four-year-old wouldn't?

Daisy made a check beside Rita and Meredith's names on the attendance sheet. "Betty?"

A chubby, round-faced girl with lank, brown hair pulled back carelessly, popped a handful of jelly beans into her mouth and raised her hand.

Stripes. Horizontal. The poor thing. She looks like a hot-air balloon about to ascend.

Daisy returned her attention to the attendance sheet. "You must be Mary Jean," she said to the girl next to Betty.

Mary Jean grunted an affirmative response as she continued to hunch over the table, thumbing through a magazine.

"And what do you expect to get from the class, Mary Jean?"

"My driver's permit." She turned the page. "My dad said I could get it if I attended Bible study."

Daisy cleared her throat. "I haven't heard anyone say she was taking the class to acquire a deeper faith, spiritual enlightenment, or a more profound understanding of the Gospels."

A groan rumbled around the table.

"Why does that not surprise me?" She tucked the attendance sheet back into the folder and pulled out a stack of mimeographed pages. "I admit, it would be more fun if there were boys in the class. And, of course, Pastor Jack is the resident Bible expert—in addition to being quite cute."

Rita blushed.

Daisy began distributing the papers. "But for the time being you'll just have to put up with me"—she glanced in Mary Jean's direction—"if you want to get your driver's permit."

Daisy turned to the group. "We'll begin next week with the book of Matthew. The sheets I passed out will help start the discussion."

"Homework?" Betty made a face, which was accompanied by more groans around the table.

"You won't be tested," Daisy assured them.

While the girls read over the introductory pages to the assignment, Daisy allowed her gaze to rest deliberately on each one. All the qualities endemic to teenage angst—sullen indifference, self-consciousness, and insecurity—were reflected in the way they held themselves and from the expressions on their faces.

Her optimistic spirit was being seriously challenged. She realized that she hadn't had an inkling as to what she was getting herself into. Once again, her impulsive nature had gotten the best of her.

"It's one minute to five," Meredith warned.

"Just enough time for a short prayer," Daisy said.

As they clasped hands around the table, she said, "We'll each pray silently to ourselves."

Daisy was a firm believer that the good Lord didn't let us dig ourselves a pit too deep to scramble out of.

With that in mind she prayed. She prayed with all her might. And as she prayed a plan began to form.

"Amen!"

four

"Well, how did your first class go?" Jack asked as he walked Daisy next door to Lou's Lube, where he'd had her car towed.

The garage and service station was on Third Street and backed up to the church parking lot.

"Very interesting." Daisy hurried along beside him taking two quick steps to every stride of his.

"What does that mean?"

"What it says."

Jack shrugged. "You don't want to tell me? Suit yourself."

She paused. "Oh, and I'll need a bigger classroom."

"You've only got six students, Daisy." Jack slowed. "Or is it five? So why do you need a bigger room?"

"You think I'm about to give away all my secrets?"

"Clearly not." He looked mildly irritated and resumed walking.

Daisy rushed to catch up. "So. Do I get the bigger room?"

"I'll see what I can do. Here we are." Jack queried the kid pumping gas. "Lou in the garage?"

The kid nodded. "Hey, Lou, somebody to see you."

Jack and Daisy skirted a pile of old tires and entered the cavernous wooden structure attached to the office.

"Be with ya in a minute." The voice coming from beneath the chassis of the small red truck sounded like dry toast.

Suddenly, a creeper shot out from under the truck in front of them. On it lay a wiry old woman with a cap of tightly permed gray hair and a wrinkled face that reflected decades of smoking.

"That's Lou?" Daisy gasped to Jack.

"What'd ja expect, a prom queen?" Lou sat up, wiping her hands on her striped denim coveralls. "Hi, P. J."

P. J.? Daisy glanced at Jack.

"Pastor Jack." He laughed, putting his hand in the small of Daisy's back. "This is Daisy Fielding, Lou, she's the owner of the—"

"Expensive bauble," Lou interrupted, giving the spiffy yellow sports car a sidelong glance. She turned to Jack. "Have to get a fuel pump. I'll have it fixed by noon tomorrow."

"*You're* going to fix it?" Daisy struggled to keep the uncertainty out of her voice.

"Afraid I'll break a fingernail?" Lou gave her the once-over, her coal-black eyes burning with challenge.

"Where's Rick?" Jack asked.

"They're fittin' him for a prosthesis at the V.A. Hospital."

Daisy didn't recall hearing Jack say that the Lou of Lou's Lube, Garage, and Service Station was a woman. According to Jack, Lou was a soft touch for the kids in the neighborhood and had hired Rick, an amputee veteran, as the main mechanic because, as Lou said, "Rick's a better mechanic with his hook than any other two mechanics put together."

Lou slid back under the truck, leaving only her head exposed. "Just gotta tighten a couple of bolts under here, and it's break time. How about hanging around for some coffee?"

"I'd like to, Lou," Jack said, "but I have some work to finish back at the office." He turned to Daisy. "Why don't you have a cup of coffee with Lou, and I'll drive you home in about a half hour."

Hanging out with Lou was not high on Daisy's priority list, but before she had a chance to demur, Jack was on his way.

"Go on into the office. This'll just take a couple a minutes," Lou said from under the truck.

Daisy, whose mantra was "Cleanliness is next to godliness," squirmed at the sight of the stereotypical service station office, dulled by a sheen of dust and grease. A battered chair was pulled up to a scarred desk that was stacked with papers, bills, telephone books, and catalogs. An old typewriter was pushed to the side, with a telephone beside it. Dirty rags were piled up in the corner.

The scent of scorched coffee wafted from the coffeepot atop an old metal filing cabinet.

The thought of consuming it made Daisy's stomach wrench.

She pulled a lace hankie from her purse and was dusting the seat of the chair where she was about to perch when a yowl from the garage grabbed her attention. She rushed out of the office to find Lou splayed out in a pool of oil, her right leg twisted beneath her.

"Lou, what happened?" Daisy knelt beside the mechanic, ignoring the grease seeping into the fabric of her pink-and-white checked skirt.

The pain contorting Lou's face hadn't affected the string of expletives pouring from her pursed lips. "I slipped on that puddle." She groaned. "Shoulda known better."

"Where does it hurt, Lou?"

"My hip. I think it's broke."

The kid who worked the pumps had run in and now stood helplessly over them. "Ugh, Lou, your leg looks weird. I'll bet it really hurts bad. My pa was in the hospital two weeks when he broke his, and it took him three months before he could walk without crutches, and even now—"

Daisy gave him a warning look. "Will you call an ambulance, please."

"Oh, yeah. Sure." The boy hustled into the office.

"Don't you worry, Lou." Daisy took off her pink cashmere sweater and laid it over Lou. She stroked the old lady's hand. "Everything's going to be all right. The ambulance will be here in a jiffy."

Lights flashing, sirens screaming, the ambulance pulled into the station a few minutes later. Two attendants jumped out. Gently, they hoisted the sweating, swearing Lou onto the stretcher. As they slid her into the back of the vehicle, she managed to yell between paroxysms of pain, "You close up, Carl. And don't forget to lock the cash register and turn off the lights. Oh, and feed the cats."

Daisy clambered in after her. The ambulance doors slammed shut, the siren blared, and they were on their way.

Out of the back window, Daisy spotted Jack, running up the street after them. As the ambulance gained speed, he gave up the chase.

She grinned at the sight of Mister Perfect, standing there helpless, out of breath, sweating, and disheveled, his arms akimbo.

He wasn't the only one who could rise to the occasion.

five

Jack stepped up to the reception desk in the hospital lobby. "I'm here to inquire about Lou Green. She was brought in a short time ago."

"Lou Green." The receptionist scanned down the sheet in front of her. "She's still in emergency. It says here she's scheduled for the next available surgery."

"Is it possible I could see her? I'm her minister."

"They might let you. Usually only the family is allowed." The woman picked up the phone. "Her granddaughter's with her now."

Granddaughter?

After a brief exchange, the receptionist replaced the phone and directed Jack to the emergency room.

Granddaughter. Walking down the hall, he suppressed a chuckle at the thought of Lou and Daisy being remotely related.

He recognized Daisy's voice coming from behind one of the curtains that separated the cubicles.

"Don't you worry, Lou, I'll handle everything. No matter how long it takes you to get back on your feet."

"What about my garden?" Lou murmured, her gravelly voice thick from the medication. "Who'll feed the cats?"

"Everybody says I have a green thumb, and animals love me," Daisy said.

"Once Rick coulda managed the station," Lou whimpered. "Still could, but since the war he don't trust himself."

"The service station and garage will continue to run without a glitch. I'll see to it. I promise."

"The bills—the money. . ." Lou's voice drifted.

"Not to worry," Daisy assured her, "I'm great with money."

Yeah, spending it. Jack couldn't believe what he was hearing. Daisy run a service station and garage? Talk about absurd.

Before she could volunteer to take over Lou's surgery, Jack pushed aside the curtain.

"Oh, Jack, finally." The relief on Daisy's face surprised him.

Lou opened her eyes and managed a wan smile, her hand fluttering in his direction.

"You tell her not to worry, Jack," Daisy said. "We'll take care of everything."

Now it was *we*.

Jack looked down at the frail figure lying on the gurney. Without all her grit and energy, Lou's body seemed to have shrunk, hardly making a ripple in the sheet that covered her. He laid his hand over hers.

As a pastor, visiting the sick was one of the most important roles he played, and one of the most emotional. Especially with people like Lou, who had no family to care for them.

Well, apparently she now had Daisy. Say what you would about the girl, her compassionate heart was as irrepressible as her optimistic spirit.

Lou's wandering gaze found his again. "I'm not a member of your congregation, P. J.," she whispered, "but maybe. . .you could say a prayer—just in case?"

"You're part of the Lord's congregation, Lou." He squeezed her hand and reached across for Daisy's. "Of course I'll say a prayer. That's why I'm here."

As Lou was wheeled into surgery, Jack and Daisy retired to the lounge to wait.

"It will be interesting to see how you manage to pull off all those promises," Jack murmured. He lowered himself next to Daisy on a couch in the corner.

"Oh, ye of little faith." Daisy gave him a withering look. "I have it all worked out. The teenagers in the church youth group will take care of the garden and the cats, and the kids who use Lou's garage to work on their cars will help Rick staff the service station. I will supervise."

"You?"

"That's right, me. After being chairman of the costume ball, this'll be a piece of cake."

"Uh-huh." Jack suspected he'd end up being the biggest slice of that cake.

"I will also pick up the mail and see that the bills are paid."

"You've never had to pay a bill in your life."

"Well, my accountant, then. But I'll see that he gets them."

Jack shook his head.

"Don't be a dud, Jack. It'll be good for the kids and good for Lou. What's being a Christian all about anyway, if not helping your neighbor?"

Jack couldn't argue with that.

By 8:30, they knew that Lou's surgery was taking longer than expected. Although the doctor had warned them that her age made things a bit more complicated.

After Jack had consumed two old issues of *Reader's Digest*, he thumbed through a dog-eared copy of *Popular Mechanics*, figuring any knowledge he picked up might be useful in view of Daisy's big plans for the garage.

Daisy yawned and curled up on the couch next to him. Almost at once, she had dozed off.

It had been a long day.

In her sleep, she slipped awkwardly across the slick back of the Naugahyde couch, her head coming to rest at an uncomfortable angle on Jack's shoulder. Twice, he gently pushed her upright and twice she sank back again. Finally he took pity on her and stretched his arm across the back of the couch. In sleep, she snuggled closer, her head resting in that cradle between his shoulder and his neck. Soft breaths sighed through her slightly parted lips.

Jack looked down at the golden curls against his dark jacket and the long lashes sweeping her freckle-dusted cheek. He couldn't help smiling. She looked as young and vulnerable as she had as a child.

But she wasn't a child.

Suddenly he was aware of the softness and warmth of her—and the tickle of her curls against his chin.

Gently, he disengaged his arm.

It was close to nine o'clock when the doctor, still

wearing his surgical scrubs, entered the waiting room.

Jack and Daisy stood as he approached them.

Daisy spoke first. "How is she doctor? Will she be all right?"

The doctor shook hands with Jack. "It was complicated, just as we expected." He removed his glasses and rubbed the bridge of his nose. "She's in recovery now. We'll monitor her through the night. As for the outcome, we'll just have to wait and see. In people her age bones don't knit as readily. But she's a tough old bird, that's in her favor."

Jack smiled. "How well we know."

The doctor looked at Daisy. "You better get this little lady home. She looks bushed," he said to Jack, then turned back to Daisy. "Get a good night's sleep. You'll be in much better shape to visit your grandmother tomorrow."

Daisy ignored Jack's beleaguered glance. "Thank you, Doctor. And thank you for bending the rules and letting me stay with her in the emergency room."

"She had quite a wait before surgery. Your being there kept her calm." The doctor slid on his glasses. "Well, I've still got rounds to make."

As soon as he'd disappeared down the hall Jack turned to Daisy. "You didn't really tell him you were Lou's granddaughter?"

"Of course not."

Typical Daisy. She would never lie, but she was not above allowing folks to draw their own inferences if it suited her purpose.

six

In the hospital parking lot, Jack slid behind the wheel of his aging Dodge and slammed the car door. He glanced at Daisy beside him. "I'll buy you dinner."

"I'd love that, Jack, but I've got to get home to Tiffany, or there'll be a major mess to clean up."

"Tiffany?"

"My dog. Didn't you know I have a dog?"

"When did that happen?" Jack put the car in gear and backed out of the parking space.

"About a month ago. God did it again. He put another homeless mutt in the middle of the street."

Jack shifted gears and turned toward the parking lot exit.

"I couldn't let her get run over. Almost got run over myself, coaxing her into the back of my car."

Jack eased into the traffic.

"I took her straight to the vet, got her her shots, had her groomed. Poor baby, she was a matted mess. Called the pound. Nobody claimed her, so she was mine."

"I thought animals weren't allowed where you live," Jack said, pulling up and stopping in front of an elegant three-story apartment complex.

"They aren't."

"So what's with Tiffany?"

"I own the building."

"Why didn't I know that?"

"You never asked. There are a lot of things you don't know about me, Jack, believe it or not."

"I'm sure there are." Although he doubted it. Daisy had been pretty much an open book to him since she was a kid.

"Why don't you come up and meet my new girlfriend."

"Tiffany?"

Daisy nodded.

"Why not?" He pulled the keys from the ignition.

They stepped from the elevator into the spacious foyer of Daisy's third-floor penthouse. It opened into an elegant, antique-filled living room. Daisy had decorated it in shades of white, setting off her pre-Columbian and contemporary art collections.

As always, Jack felt slightly uneasy in the opulent surroundings. They reflected Daisy and Court's upbringing but were acutely foreign to his own humble background.

But this time he didn't have long to ponder the point for suddenly a huge dog hurtled around the corner from the hall. Balancing on its hind legs, it rested its two front paws on Jack's chest and commenced depositing wet, slurping kisses all over his face.

Jack reared back.

"She likes you, Jack." Daisy grabbed the dog's collar. "Down, girl."

Tiffany flattened on the tile floor, her jowls spreading on either side of her crossed paws as she fixed large, soulful eyes on Jack.

"She's still a puppy," Daisy said, apologetically. "She isn't completely trained yet."

"Some puppy." Jack brushed the long, clinging hairs from his dark jacket. "With a name like Tiffany, I somehow expected something smaller."

"Just goes to show you never should jump to conclusions." Daisy threw her arms around the dog's neck and nuzzled her ruff. "Good girl, Tiffany. Isn't she adorable?"

"One of God's creatures." *Actually, a combination of God's creatures*, Jack mused silently, observing the bloodhound's loose skin, otter tail, low-slung ears, and the pointed nose and long hair of a border collie.

"I knew you'd love her." Daisy opened the door to the guest closet and pulled a leash off a hook. "She needs to do her business. I'll be right back."

"Let me," Jack said, taking the leash and attaching it to Tiffany's collar.

"You really want to?"

"Can't wait. You have had a long day. Go put your feet up."

In the elevator Tiffany sat primly beside Jack, panting with anticipation. Once out on the sidewalk it was a different story. Yanking on the leash she charged, sniffing, pausing, and circling, seeking the perfect spot. No rock, tree, or fire hydrant on the block went unexplored. It was all Jack could do to keep her from dashing into the street and herding the passing automobiles.

Hard to imagine how petite little Daisy managed this mammoth, exuberant beast.

Tiffany was but another in Daisy's long list of follies.

All her life she'd been collecting strays, animals. . .people. Even when she was young and lived with her grandmother and had to hide them in the garage: abandoned kitties, the homeless boy, a lost turtle.

Both Jack and Tiffany were panting when they returned. As they got off the elevator, a whiff of provocative scents wafted from the kitchen.

Tiffany jerked free. She raced into the kitchen and plopped down in front of Daisy, affixing her with an unblinking stare.

Daisy looked up from cracking an egg. "Were you a good girl, Tiffany?"

"Depends on your definition of good." Jack leaned down and unhooked the dog's leash.

"Get in your bed," Daisy commanded, cutting a generous piece of ham from the slices in the frying pan.

Tiffany trotted over to the huge basket in the corner.

"Now, you stay," she said, giving Tiffany the meat.

Daisy had on a fancy flowered apron with a ruffled bib and looked as pretty and perky as an ad in that women's magazine she'd given Jack at Feingold's Deli.

"What are you grinning at, Jack?"

"Nothing." He draped the leash around his neck. "I thought you were going to put your feet up." He gravitated to the stove and was about to check the contents of the oven when Daisy grabbed a wooden spoon and lightly slapped his hand.

"Don't you dare. The popovers will fall."

"Popovers?" Obediently he moved back. "You *have* been busy."

He leaned against the columned arch that separated the kitchen from the dining room, his gaze following Daisy as she moved efficiently about her gourmet-equipped kitchen. She wasn't Ditsi Daisy in the kitchen, that was for sure. The girl had elevated her hobby from mere cooking to culinary art. "I planned to feed you, and here you're doing all this fussing."

"If scrambled eggs and fried ham are fussing, you're easily impressed." She added a couple of tablespoons of water to the whisked eggs.

"I thought you were supposed to add cream."

"Not in the cooking school I went to. Cream makes scrambled eggs tough. Water keeps them soft and fluffy." From a small container, she dropped in a half teaspoon of a thick yellow liquid. "Truffle oil," she said, responding to his questioning gaze.

"Aren't truffles the fungus that the pigs dig up in France?"

"Don't turn up your nose, Jack, they're a great delicacy."

"And expensive."

"So what? I can afford them." Her tone was belligerent.

He frowned. Daisy knew how he felt about spending money on frivolous indulgences such as truffles when there were so many people starving. Especially when in a few swallows they were gone.

Now was not the time to get into that discussion with her. "What can I do to help?"

"I thought we'd eat on the patio."

"I'll set the table."

Just outside the dining room's French doors, a small

round café table with two matching chairs was nestled between potted ficus trees and flowering plants in a corner of the balcony. In the center of the table a candle glowed beside a nosegay of pink baby roses in a cut glass vase.

"This all seems a bit fancy for ham and eggs," Jack called, putting down the place mats. "I hope you didn't go to all this trouble on my account."

There was a beat of silence. Then Daisy said, "Don't flatter yourself, Jack. Even when I'm alone I find everything tastes better if it's attractively served."

She brought out a teapot, steeping, and two china cups. "Sit down; everything's almost ready."

Tiffany lumbered in from the kitchen and lay down under the table, resting her jowls on Jack's foot.

Jack sensed he had hurt Daisy's feelings, or at least irritated her. He was sorry about that. What in the past had been an easy, open relationship had become strained. He'd begun to notice it after she returned from her extended vacation in the east. Just before Court and Rebecca's wedding. Something must have happened on that trip. One of these days he'd find out what it was.

Daisy returned with a tray bearing their plates of a scrumptious-looking array of scrambled eggs, ham, a slice of fresh pineapple, and a sprig of parsley. Also on the tray, a covered basket of hot popovers, a crock of sweet butter, and a covered crystal bowl of what appeared to be homemade strawberry jam.

"Looks delicious," Jack said with amazed enthusiasm

as she placed his plate in front of him. He sniffed. "And smells even better."

"And all the food groups are represented," Daisy said, sliding into the chair across from him. "Well, I've done my part, now it's your turn."

She reached for his hand, and they bowed their heads.

Jack prayed, "Thank You, Lord, for the food we are about to eat and the hands that prepared it. As we enjoy this excessive bounty, may we always be mindful of the needs of those who do not share our privilege. Amen."

"Short and sweet." Daisy picked up her fork. "Just so you know, Jack, your little sermon was not lost on me. Excessive bounty. Really." She popped a forkful of scrambled eggs into her mouth, chewed, and swallowed. "I hardly call a half teaspoonful of truffle oil excessive. I refuse to feel guilty."

"That wasn't my intention." Jack broke open a steaming popover, slathered it with butter and strawberry jam, and took a generous bite.

"Don't tell me that. Lately, it's always your intention."

He prudently changed the subject. This food was too delicious to waste. "These popovers are terrific."

"Thank you. Clearly, you're very uncomfortable with the way I spend my money. Like buying truffles. You never miss an opportunity to make the point."

"Forget the truffles, Daisy. Your food tastes great."

"They're just an example." She sliced a bite of ham. "Everybody knows ministers live on what comes out of the collection plate. Nobody thinks about it. Nobody cares." She looked up at him. "Except maybe the minister. Nobody judges you on it because that's just the way it is. You have no choice."

She just doesn't get it. "I could have chosen a different line of work."

"Like professional football player."

"I almost did."

She gave a cocky tilt to her head. "But of course you didn't because then you might have gotten rich." Her sarcasm turned serious. "You know, sometimes I think you wear financial deprivation as if it were a badge of honor."

Jack refused to take the bait. He returned a bland gaze. " 'Lay not up for yourselves treasures upon earth, where moth and rust doth corrupt.' That's my motto," he said, quoting Matthew 6:19.

She pointed her knife at him. "But if somebody lives off a trust fund they're bad or lazy or whatever."

"Not bad."

"Well, not good." She crossed her knife and fork on the plate. "It doesn't matter what else they do or how generous their contributions, it's never enough."

The woman is determined to ruin this meal. He took another bite of the exceptional eggs.

She glared at him. "The point is, Jack, I didn't have a choice. I was born rich. Does that mean I shouldn't enjoy it? I should give away all the antiques I inherited from my grandmother and my collection of Puma Dogs and the paintings I was able to purchase—most of them from poor, struggling artists, I might add. In some quarters, I'm even considered a patron."

"Daisy, your food is getting cold."

"Just one more thing, and then I'll be quiet. I don't appreciate it when you look down your nose at my friends, either—"

"I never—"

"Oh yes, you do. You automatically assume that if someone is rich, they lack compassion."

For several minutes there was silence between them.

Daisy glanced away. "It's gotten so sometimes I wonder why I—"

"Why you what?"

"Why I—why I even. . .like you."

Jack looked into her tear-brimmed eyes, shimmering in the candlelight.

His heart tightened.

Had his thoughts about Daisy and her country club set been that transparent?

He could deny it 'til the cows came home, but Daisy knew him too well. Regardless of what he thought about them, they were Daisy's friends, and she cared about them.

He felt terrible.

Some minister I am. He'd preached Matthew 7:1, "Judge not, that ye be not judged," but when it came to Daisy, he did just the opposite. He took the same proprietary role now that he'd taken when she was a little girl.

The candlelight danced over her face, the hollows of her cheeks, her downcast eyes, and the gentle curve of her neck.

He took a deep breath.

She wasn't a little girl anymore. She was a woman, and she had a right to make her own choices and decisions.

"I'm sorry, Daisy." He leaned forward and reached for her hand. It was warm and soft, and lay lightly in his. "Of all the people I don't want to hurt, it's you."

Daisy didn't answer.

"I'm glad you told me how you feel. I'm going to take it very seriously. I certainly don't want to be the kind of judgmental person you just described."

Tiffany stirred and stood, leaning against Jack's leg. Jack scratched behind her ears. "I'm a work in progress, too, Tiffany."

"We all are," Daisy said quietly.

"With the Lord's help. . . ."

seven

Daisy leaned against the open elevator door, feeling a twinge of guilt. "I'm sorry I was such a harridan."

"No, Daisy. You gave me something to think about." He smiled, patting Tiffany's head as the dog nudged between them. "Isn't that what friends are supposed to do?"

"Well, then I was certainly a good friend tonight." She looked down at Tiffany. "She's really bonded with you. Do you think she's partial to all men, or just you?"

Jack smiled. "Thanks for the supper. I hadn't had time for lunch and—" A stricken look crossed his face. "Oh, no! I was supposed to have dinner with Court and Rebecca tonight."

"Me, too. But not to worry. I called them from the hospital and told them I wasn't coming, and I doubted that you would be either."

Jack shook his head with relief. "God bless you."

"Don't mention it." Daisy straightened. "About tomorrow. What time does the gas station open?"

"I think Rick usually opens it at about seven."

"Since you're so close, can you meet him there and tell him about Lou?"

"I was planning to."

"Martha gets here about eight, so I can leave any time after that."

"I thought that your cleaning lady only came on Mondays."

"She used to, but now she comes five days a week. Her mother needed an operation for which Martha, of course, didn't have the money. I insisted on paying for it, but she insisted she wouldn't take charity. So now she comes every day. I didn't need her in the beginning, but with Tiffany shedding and drooling all over the house, I'm kind of glad she does."

Daisy suppressed a yawn and began ticking off the things to be done the next day. "First thing, I'll see about getting help at the garage. Then we can check on the cats and see what else needs to be done at Lou's house. Oh, by the way, it occurred to me that instead of a classroom, what I really need for my Bible study group is the fellowship hall."

"Daisy—"

"If it's not being used, what's the difference?"

Jack gave a beleaguered sigh.

"I knew you'd agree."

He folded his arms across his chest. "You know, Daisy, you missed your calling. You should have been a marine drill sergeant."

"Is that a compliment, Jack?"

"Of course, Ditsi." He patted her arm, stepped into the elevator, and pushed the down button. "I'll pick you up tomorrow at eight thirty," he called out as the door slid shut.

Daisy and Tiffany stood in the foyer, listening to the whirr of the elevator's descent.

Daisy sighed.

"Well, at least he didn't pat me on the head like he used to do when I was a kid," she murmured.

Tiffany leaned against the elevator door and whimpered softly.

"Already you miss him. Me, too."

❧

The next morning, Jack dropped Daisy at Lou's Lube on his way to the board meeting of Ecumenical Family Services, of which he was the chairman. "I'll be back in a couple of hours."

Daisy waved him off and turned to the mechanic.

Rick was long and lanky and had a kind of hangdog look as he slouched against the fender of her yellow car. In place of a left hand he had a hook. In it he grasped an oily rag, deftly wiping grease from between the fingers of his remaining hand.

His pockmarked face was sad. "I can't believe it. Poor old Lou. I hope she's gonna be all right."

"We're praying for that," Daisy said. "We'll know more when we talk to the doctor this afternoon."

Rick's tough expression softened. "Lou's like a mother to me, ya know. She and Harry took me in when I was a kid on the streets. I don't know where I'd be without 'em." He looked away. A hint of tears shimmered in his drooping gray eyes. "Harry taught me everything about being a mechanic. A course nobody could take Harry's place, but when he died I did my best to help Lou out. Then the war came."

He sighed. "I was a mechanic in the army 'til I got my hand blowed off. But good old Lou. She had my job waiting. Not many folks woulda done that for a one-handed mechanic."

"Lou says you're the best," Daisy said.

"She's the best. I'll do anything to help her out."

"I've made a list. Why don't we go inside and talk it over?" Daisy suggested.

"Good idea." Rick led the way into the office where he used his oily rag to wipe off the seat of Lou's scarred desk chair for Daisy.

"You're a gentleman of the old school, Rick," Daisy said, hesitating for only an instant before sitting down in her new blue silk dress.

She crossed her legs and pulled a small notebook and pencil from her purse.

"The first thing we have to do is get you some help here at the garage while Lou's convalescing. Maybe a couple of the kids she lets tinker with their cars might be interested in a summer job."

"I can think a two or three that might." Rick frowned. "But I don't know if Lou can afford it, with her being sick and all."

"I'll worry about the money," Daisy said. "What do you think we should pay them?"

"Well, let's see. I make a dollar an hour. A course Lou's real generous with me."

"Seventy-five cents an hour for them?"

"Sounds about right."

"Six days a week from seven until seven. Right?"

Rick nodded.

"I'm going to leave it up to you, Rick. You know what you need and who would be best to fill it."

"Reckon I do."

Daisy ticked jobs and wages off in her notebook. "What about the daily receipts?"

"I usually close up and put the money and receipts in the safe. Lou balances the books and makes the bank deposit Monday morning."

"That and payroll will be my job." Actually it would be her accountant's job.

She made another check on the sheet and looked up. "Do you by any chance know where there's a key to Lou's house? I promised I'd collect the mail, and I thought I'd gather some things she might need in the hospital."

"She keeps a key under the mat. Sometimes I go in and feed the cats for her."

"Would you? It would be great help if I could count on you for that," Daisy said, "since you're here every day."

"Be glad to." Rick was looking downright cocky at all the additional responsibility with which he was being entrusted.

"Well, that's taken care of." Daisy snapped the notebook closed and dropped it back into her purse. She stood up and reached for Rick's grease-stained hand. "You're a real blessing, Rick. To Lou and all of us. It's a great relief to know there's someone here that can be counted on."

Rick took her hand. The pride in his face at the compliment almost made her want to cry.

Out behind the garage, the back half of Lou's property was a jungle of weeds, half-dead trees, and carcasses of abandoned cars. A broken-down picket fence separated it from Lou's thriving vegetable garden and white box-framed house, with its blue door and blue-trimmed shutters, standing amidst a tangle of vines and flowers.

With its flower boxes and garden statues of deer, ducks, and gnomes, the little house looked loved, but as Daisy climbed the rickety front stairs and stepped onto the porch, she realized the property was in serious disrepair. It needed more than a good coat of paint, although that would have been a move in the right direction. Boards rippled on the front porch, shutters sagged, and the porch railing was so loose it was downright dangerous.

When she reached under the frayed mat for the key, she drew back in disgust. Worms and maggots writhed in the damp rectangle beneath it. She pulled a perfumed lace hankie from her purse and gingerly picked up the key. Wiping it carefully, she fitted it into the lock.

Two fat, well-groomed brown and white calicos met her at the door, the bells on their collars tinkling as they snaked around her silk-stockinged legs, purring a friendly greeting. Daisy reached down and scratched them each behind the ears.

The tiny house had the musty smell of years of stored memories.

A blue plaid sofa and two mismatched chairs flanked

the faux fireplace. In front of it stood a three-tiered scratching post. On the coffee table were piles of photographs, several magazines and dog-eared dime novels, and stacks of old newspapers.

Daisy shook her head at the clutter. It was about as opposite from her own pristine apartment as she could imagine.

Her gaze lifted to the ornately framed hand-colored wedding photograph of a much younger Lou and her husband, Harry, hanging above the knickknack-crowded mantel. She couldn't help comparing it with the modern paintings gracing her own walls. Her eyes grew misty. There was no doubt which held the greater value.

When she went into the kitchen to feed the cats, she was not surprised that time had taken its toll there, too, in the crud-laden corners and equipment chipped and tarnished. Once white walls were stained with years of smoke and grease.

And then her gaze fell on a large Mason jar sitting in the middle of the blue oilcloth covering the table. It was filled with roses, carnations, petunias, salvia, and drooping honeysuckle that Lou must have picked from her garden the day before. Daisy saw the cats' blue china dishes, inscribed with their names—Betty and Boots—on the floor by the sink. The kitchen window was open just wide enough for Lou's beloved kitties to go in and out.

Once again, Daisy knew she had glimpsed the heart of the woman.

As Daisy gave the little two-bedroom, one-bath house a final quick perusal, a plan began to form. By the time she had locked the front door and returned the key to its place beneath the mat, she knew what she was going to do.

A few minutes later, when she met Jack in front of the garage, the only thing she had taken from Lou's house was the beautiful arrangement of flowers.

No florist shop's formal bouquet could compare with those from Lou's own garden.

eight

"The flowers are beautiful, but Lou needs her tooth-brush," Jack said as Daisy clambered into his Dodge with the bouquet from Lou's garden.

"I thought we could pick up one at Walster's Department Store on our way to the hospital." She rolled down the window and waved at Rick. "See you later."

Jack shifted gears and stepped on the accelerator. "Who buys toothbrushes at an elegant department store?"

"I do. Among other things Lou's going to need."

"What she needs? Or what *you* think she needs?"

Daisy adjusted the Mason jar of flowers in her lap. "Don't be a grump, Jack. It won't take long. I know where everything is."

"I'll bet you do," he mumbled irritably, stopping at a red light.

"Besides, it's hardly out of our way," she said.

A half hour later Daisy had not only purchased a toothbrush, toothpaste, mouthwash, and floss, but a quilted satin pouch to hold them. She had also chosen a manicure kit.

"Manicures and pedicures really give you a lift when you're sick."

She bought an extra-large jar of body cream and

perfume, a bed jacket, two silk nightgowns, a down-filled robe, and matching slippers.

"For when she's in the convalescent hospital." Daisy paused in the middle of the lingerie department and looked around. "I'm sure there's something I've forgotten."

"I find that hard to believe," Jack grumbled, adjusting the boxes he was carrying.

"Now I remember." Unfazed, Daisy brightened. "Bed socks."

"I hope that's it, Daisy. It's twelve thirty. I'm getting hungry."

"You've been such a good sport, I'm taking you to lunch," Daisy said, pondering which bed socks to purchase.

"No. You made dinner last night. I'm taking you."

"I have a special place in mind." She handed her choice to the salesgirl.

"That's all right. It's my turn."

"Please. Besides, it won't cost me anything. I'm going to charge it."

"Daisy—"

"Don't make a scene, Jack. It's not becoming. Especially in a man of the cloth." Daisy winked at the salesgirl, adding the bed socks to Jack's pile. "Upstairs there's a lovely tearoom."

"Tearoom?"

☙

Ninety minutes later they were on their way to the hospital.

"I told you they served lunch," Daisy said. "And it was

quicker than getting in the car and having to drive some-place and park, and then maybe having to wait. We'll be at the hospital right at the start of visiting hours."

"The club sandwich wasn't bad," Jack conceded, turn-ing into the parking lot. "Neither was that tall, exotic-looking raven-haired model with the flashing dark eyes."

He grinned at Daisy.

Daisy sniffed. "The redhead wasn't too shabby, either. It was shameless, though, the way she threw herself at you. And you a minister."

"Funny, I didn't notice."

"You're so naive." She gave him a sidelong look. "Or were you trying to make me jealous?"

"You know me better than that, Daisy."

Yes, she did.

No wonder the models hovered, he was such a striking study in contrasts: solemn black suit and clerical collar, laughing eyes, and teasing smile. He couldn't help it. It was just the way he was.

She sighed. "I'm forced to admit it, Jack, even I could see you were the handsomest man in the room."

"The only one without a cane." He swung into a parking place and stopped.

She smiled. She honestly didn't think he knew how terribly attractive he was. Which was also a tremen-dously appealing quality. "You were a good sport, Jack, and you handled yourself very well."

Jack grinned. "Got my training at the ladies' guild luncheons at church."

He hopped out of the car, sprinted around to the

passenger side, and opened the door for Daisy. She handed him Lou's flowers and leaned over the seat, riffling through the parcels in back.

"I think we'll just take her toothbrush, toothpaste, and the body cream this trip. I want to give her a pedicure, but that can wait until the convalescent hospital."

When Daisy and Jack entered Lou's room, her eyes were closed and a nurse was slipping ice chips between her parched lips. She looked so small and helpless lying there, tubes coming out of her nose and arm.

At least she didn't have to share a room. Daisy had seen to that.

The nurse looked up and gave a silent nod as Daisy deposited the things she'd brought in a chair by the door. She took the flowers from Jack and tiptoed over, setting them in the windowsill where Lou would see them when she opened her eyes—which she did at that moment—small slits, and turned her head, clamping her mouth shut against the spoon of ice chips.

"You don't want any more?"

Lou shook her head slightly.

"Very well." The nurse dropped the spoon back into the glass of ice chips and set it on the chest beside the bed. "You have some visitors, Mrs. Green," she said, rising. "I'll be back in a few minutes to check on you." Her rubber-soled shoes squished softly as she crossed the slick linoleum floor.

Daisy and Jack moved to the bed, Jack on one side, Daisy on the other, dropping into the chair the nurse had just vacated.

"Don't talk, dear," Daisy murmured, stroking Lou's arm as the old woman struggled to focus on her. "We just came by to see how you are and if there's anything you need." Reaching up, she smoothed her hand over Lou's brow.

Her skin felt leathery and feverish.

Jack leaned down and spoke softly. "Daisy's taken care of everything, Lou. You don't have to worry about a thing." He took Lou's small gnarled hand in his and held it so gently and caressed it, as if he had rescued an injured sparrow.

Daisy looked at him across the bed, the contrast of his dark suit against the pristine white of the sheets. He seemed so solid and trustworthy, like a big, comforting angel. His wheat-colored hair was a bit disheveled, as it always was, his dark eyes warm and compassionate.

She felt wrapped in such peace, as if she could see her whole life stretching out in front of her. She and Jack together, visiting the sick.

It was a delirious moment.

"You're on the prayer chain at church," Jack said.

Lou's parched lips began to move.

Daisy and Jack leaned closer.

Her whisper was dry as a dead leaf. "Prayers must be workin'. Rigor mortis ain't set in yet."

nine

Two weeks later, Jack and Daisy were to meet for lunch to discuss what they were going to do about Lou Green. Jack glanced impatiently at the clock on his desk.

They were supposed to have met yesterday, but Daisy had canceled. He'd been disappointed and realized, to his surprise, how much he'd been looking forward to his dose of Daisy sunshine.

Mrs. Beemer's voice crackled over the intercom. "Daisy's here."

A rush of pleasure surged through him. "I'll be right out."

She was perched on the edge of Mrs. Beemer's desk in a pink-and-white polka-dot sleeveless dress, swinging one small, sandaled foot. A pink ribbon tied back her golden curls.

Jack smiled. Pink had been her favorite color as far back as he could remember. Scraped knees and pretty in pink. That had been Daisy.

She must have just said something that made Mrs. Beemer laugh.

It was good to see the heavyset, gray-haired church secretary laughing. Mrs. Beemer was a Gold Star mother, a widow, whose only son had been killed near the end of the war. She'd found little to laugh or even smile about since.

Jack had made her a special target of his prayers.

Daisy looked up and gave him a twinkling smile. "I have a surprise." Her cheeks were rosy, and her blue eyes sparkled. "I'm driving."

"Your driving is always fraught with surprise," Jack said. *And terror*, he wanted to add.

"It's time you stopped stereotyping women drivers, Jack. Isn't that right, Mrs. Beemer?"

"Not all women drivers," Jack defended. "Just you."

Mrs. Beemer smiled. "I'm too smart to take sides."

"You would if you'd ever driven with her." Jack grinned at Daisy.

She jumped down from the desk. "Well, if I'm a bad driver you have only yourself and Court to blame. You're the ones who taught me." She grabbed his hand and dragged him toward the door.

Truth be told, he didn't offer much resistance.

"Don't forget, you have a one thirty appointment," Mrs. Beemer called after them.

As they hurried out into the parking lot, Daisy said, "We're going on a picnic."

The top was down on her little yellow car, and she scrambled into the driver's seat before Jack could be a gentleman and open the door. As he got in on the other side, she leaned over and pulled a pair of super-sized sunglasses from the glove compartment. Putting them on, she drew back, struck a pose, and flashed a toothy smile. "What do you think of my new shades? I bought them in New York. They were on sale."

"You look like a movie star."

"Perfect." She inserted the key into the ignition and revved the engine.

Jack flinched as she stripped gears.

The car lurched forward, barreled out of the parking lot, and swung left on York Boulevard.

A few minutes later, Daisy was inching along the curb of a small park. She jerked to a stop in the one clear spot that wasn't under a tree. "So the birds won't make a deposit on my new automobile." Giggling as if the joke were new, she swung out of the car and reached into the backseat for a blanket and her briefcase.

"Some briefcase," Jack said, lifting out the picnic basket.

"Isn't it chic? I was with a friend at the luggage store, and there it was in the front window, crying, 'Buy me, buy me, I match your alligator shoes.'"

A tousled, red-haired boy ran between them, chasing what appeared to be his smaller red-haired sister.

Daisy stepped aside, knocking into a piñata swinging near a table festooned with crepe paper and bouquets of balloons. Seated around the table was a cadre of small birthday revelers in pointy hats with milky mustaches and chocolate lips.

"You ought to come here on a weekend. It's a zoo," she said cheerfully.

The few scattered tables were mostly occupied by young mothers, maybe a grandmother or two, chatting as they kept one eye on the children. A uniformed nanny pushed her twin charges on the swings, while nearby, three little girls took turns going hand over hand across bars.

Daisy found an out-of-the-way spot and spread the large, gray blanket on the sun-dappled grass in the shade of leaning sycamores.

Jack put down the picnic basket and took off his jacket, laid it on a corner of the blanket, and stretched out beside it. Crossing his ankles and locking his hands behind his head, he closed his eyes. For a moment he let the hypnotic tinkle of the children's laughter and the warm, caressing breeze lull him into a pleasant state of euphoria.

Through half-lidded eyes he saw a butterfly settle for an instant on the sleeve of his jacket and then fly away.

"Some folks might think that meant good luck was on its way." Daisy smiled at him and opened the picnic basket.

"Mmm," was all the response he could muster.

He watched her bring out small, artistically arranged platters of exotic cheeses, sliced pâté—"The meat loaf of France," she informed him—gourmet crackers, a basket of fresh fruit, and chocolate truffles for dessert. "Since you're so fond of truffles."

A man could get used to this.

His stomach was beginning to grumble. He grinned and sat up.

Daisy passed him a china plate and poured him iced tea from a thermos into a cut glass goblet, no less.

After Jack blessed their food, she spread a linen napkin

on her lap and looked up. "By the way, I'm not eight years old anymore. I'd just as soon you and my brother would refrain from calling me Ditsi. At least to my face."

"Oh, come on, Daisy. It's a term of endearment."

She lifted a skeptical brow.

"Really." He gave her his most engaging grin. "Would a minister lie?"

Her look told him she knew that he thought of her as frivolous, but it didn't mean he should consider her a fool.

She probably understood him as well as he did her. Maybe better. Worse, she had a very astute and silent way of laying on the guilt. She was so good-natured most of the time that when she did, he figured he deserved it.

He put down his plate. "I'm sorry, Daisy. I won't call you that anymore if it hurts your feelings."

Daisy broke off a cluster of grapes. "It's demeaning."

"That certainly wasn't my intention. I admit, sometimes you seem like the butterfly that landed on my jacket." He smiled and took her hand. "But you're as straight a thinker and well organized as anyone I know. So if I forget and call you Ditsi sometimes, it's only because—"

"I know, it's a term of endearment." She withdrew her hand.

Jack didn't want to let it get away. But it was only a momentary lapse. This was little Daisy, after all, way too young and way too flighty—for all her virtues—for a man in his line of work.

Daisy snapped open her briefcase and brought out the list she'd compiled of all the things that needed to be done to fix Lou's house. While eating lunch they discussed them.

The garden, the roof, the porch floor and rail, a coat of paint—inside and out—new linoleum in the bathroom and kitchen, et cetera, et cetera, et cetera. "And I'm afraid we may have to build her a ramp. Even if she's not in a wheelchair, stairs will be difficult."

"That's a lot to accomplish." Jack tried not to sound too skeptical as he spread Brie on a cracker.

"It is, but I think most of it can be done in a couple of weekends if enough folks pitch in." She handed him a sheet of paper. "What do you think of the schedule I've made?"

Jack looked at it and began to laugh. "You think this is the way teenage boys want to spend their Saturday?"

"If girls are there."

"Why would teenage girls want to paint and weed and lay linoleum?"

"If boys are there."

"And you'll be in charge?"

Daisy nodded.

Jack looked down at her soft, slender hands. "Think of what it will do to your manicure."

"Nothing, if I wear gloves."

"Looks like you've thought of everything, *Sergeant* Daisy."

"Another term of endearment?" She popped a grape in her mouth.

"Of course."

What could he say to that? Retreating to the safety of the meal, he and Daisy spent the next several moments eating in silence. . .a companionable silence.

When they had finished, Daisy put away her lists and began to repack the picnic basket.

"How's the Bible study class going?" Jack remembered to ask.

"Oh, fine." She wrapped the crystal goblets in their napkins and tucked them carefully on top.

"I can't remember. How long have you been meeting?"

"About five weeks."

"That long. How many are enrolled?"

"Oh, between. . ." Her answer was muffled as she reached down to pick up the blanket.

"How many?"

"Oh, I guess eighteen or twenty," she said, her manner offhand.

"Eighteen or twenty?"

"Well, maybe twenty-five sometimes."

"Twenty-five. Daisy, that's amazing."

Jack waited for Daisy to continue, but she gathered up her briefcase and the blanket and started toward the car.

It wasn't like Daisy to be so evasive. Maybe it was because of their wager. Maybe she just didn't want to tip her hand.

But, why? She'd already won.

He picked up the picnic basket and followed her.

A gust of wind lifted the hem of her skirt, giving him

a glimpse of shapely calf and thoughts of Daisy that were new to him—and not at all brotherly.

He pushed them aside.

ten

Daisy's high voltage always left Jack in a breathless rush. He sprinted into his office after their lunch, barely on time for his 1:30 appointment.

Mrs. Beemer looked up from the mimeograph machine. "No need to hurry, Ray and Suzie had to change their appointment until Saturday morning. Ray had an emergency at work and couldn't get away." Mrs. Beemer straightened the stack of papers. "It's always interesting as to what qualifies a bachelor to give prenuptial counseling."

Jack tossed her a beleaguered look. They'd been through similar exchanges many times. Mrs. Beemer did not feel she had done her job unless she'd inserted a dig about his single status when an opportunity arose.

"You ought to get yourself a wife, Pastor," she said.

"When the right woman comes along." He picked up the mail from the basket on her desk.

"How do you know she hasn't?"

"If you mean who I think you mean—"

"All I can say is, we both feel a lot happier when she's around."

"Everyone feels happier when Daisy is around. She's a wonderful person, but that's not a criterion for marriage."

"I certainly think it is. At least one of them." Mrs. Beemer touched the ledger on her desk and chuckled. "And I'll bet she could afford to replace that old stove in the fellowship hall kitchen."

Jack laughed. "Mrs. Beemer, I'm shocked!"

Daisy really had done a number on the church secretary this morning. Her high spirits had remained even after the girl was gone. That part was good.

"You know me," Mrs. Beemer said, adopting a scratchy, singsong voice. "I'm only thinking of what's best for the church."

Jack looked up from sorting the letters. "You sound like—"

"Mavis Parrott. But I don't have the same candidate in mind."

Jack couldn't suppress a grin. "Virginia Parrott is a fine young woman."

"There's nothing wrong with Virgie Parrott that a few hundred miles between her and her mother wouldn't cure."

"Now, now, Mrs. Beemer, be charitable."

"Incidentally, she called while you were out."

"Virgie or her mother?"

"Guess." Mrs. Beemer went into her imitation again. " 'You know I mind my own business, but. . . You know I never gossip, but. . . You know I never interfere, but. . .' That old bird always has something to squawk about."

Mrs. Beemer had a point. Mavis Parrot held strong opinions about everything and a compulsion to express them that bordered on religious obligation.

"What ruffled her feathers today?"

"Says she's been hearing troublesome rumors about the girls' Bible study group and wants to discuss them with you."

"Uh-oh."

"Truth is, she was miffed when you didn't choose Virgie to take over the class. Can you imagine how long that would have lasted? Poor, shy Virgie, those girls would have devoured her in seconds." Mrs. Beemer pulled a file from a drawer in her desk. "You made the right choice, Pastor, choosing Daisy. Look at this."

Jack's breath caught. Daisy had underestimated the enrollment when she'd said twenty-five girls. The attendance record reflected a number closer to thirty-five.

He couldn't believe it. "Do they all attend regularly?"

Mrs. Beemer nodded. "Tuesdays and Thursdays, three to five."

"Bible study only meets once a week."

"I guess Daisy thought that since it's summer. . ." Mrs. Beemer sat down and busied herself at her desk—not meeting Jack's eye, he noticed.

Which intensified his growing sense of apprehension.

He struggled with a mix of conflicting emotions: elation at the amazing attendance record and foreboding that Mrs. Parrott might be right to be concerned.

Something was beginning to smell fishy—which had nothing to do with the menu he'd planned for Daisy's wager-winning dinner.

Although that was a reason for concern, too.

He looked at Mrs. Beemer. "Do you know something

I don't but should?"

Mrs. Beemer shook her head.

The woman looked too innocent.

Clever Daisy. The hours the girls met were the same hours as the boys' interchurch Bible study and basketball league that he coached.

Jack pointed to the stack of papers Mrs. Beemer had been running off on the mimeograph machine and now was shoving hastily into a folder. "What are those?"

"Oh, just some handouts for Daisy's class."

"May I see them?" He reached across her and picked up the top sheet.

"This is a list of beauty products!"

"Oops. Wrong stack." Clearly flustered, Mrs. Beemer grabbed the paper back.

"Where is the right stack?"

"Here." She handed him a pile of pale yellow mimeographed sheets. "Bible study questions. See?"

It gave Jack a small perverse pleasure, definitely unbecoming a minister, to see her squirm under his scrutiny. Clearly she was a willing conspirator in one of Daisy's devious plots.

Jack was about to find out what it was.

❧

The next day Jack finished the boys' Bible study class and slipped out early, leaving Tim Jackson, rector of Hope Trinity, in charge of basketball practice. He entered Good Shepherd Community through the back entrance and made his way quietly down the hall. He had not even apprised Mrs. Beemer of his mission.

As he approached the fellowship hall he heard a murmur of voices punctuated by intermittent peals of laughter.

Even though he didn't put much store in Mrs. Parrott's rumor reports, that, coupled with Mrs. Beemer's obvious subterfuge and Daisy's own evasiveness yesterday, had given him reason for concern. Especially considering his own personal experience with Daisy's independent and unorthodox behavior.

It wasn't that he didn't trust her. . .

Well, he didn't. Not completely.

It wasn't that her instincts weren't good, or that she didn't have the best intentions. It was just that sometimes her flights of fancy got the best of her—and everybody else in her wake. Himself included.

Personally, for the most part, he found Ditsi Daisy's antics charming. But he had Good Shepherd Community Church to consider.

He stood with his hand on the doorknob, listening to the hubbub of happy voices.

It certainly sounded positive.

A twinge of guilt at his stealth seeped into his thoughts but was quickly dismissed. After all, he reasoned, it wasn't just the church he was considering, it was Daisy. He wanted to spare her embarrassment and the disapproval of the church board, of which Mrs. Parrott was the very outspoken treasurer.

Slowly he opened the door.

His mouth gaped open.

Groups of teenage girls crowded the room, their

energy blasting, the clamor of their excited voices, deafening.

Not a Bible in sight.

Daisy had done it again!

Appalled, Jack stepped back into the hall and closed the door.

"Jack!"

He spun around.

She stood behind him, her blue gaze burning. "What are you doing here?"

eleven

"What am *I* doing here?" After a second of guilt for being caught spying, Jack's anger erupted. "A better question would be, what are *you* doing in *there*?" He gestured toward the fellowship hall.

Daisy's face reflected uncertainty.

Good.

"Er. . .lots of things," she stammered.

"Obviously. None of which includes Bible study, however."

"No more than *basketball* looks like Bible study," Daisy snapped, a note of belligerence in her voice.

"That's your defense?"

"I didn't know I needed a defense." Her flushed cheeks told him otherwise.

He was aware of the girls' muffled, happy voices in the background.

"Come on, Daisy. If you'd thought you were doing something I'd approve of, you'd have talked about it plenty."

Her gaze shifted. "I didn't think you'd understand."

"Try me." He struggled for a benign expression while praying for the Lord to help him to keep his temper.

"Well. . ." Daisy looked down, then back up at Jack.

"It was clear from the first minute that these girls didn't have any style."

He looked heavenward and let out a breath of air.

"*Certainly* no manners." Daisy played with the pearls at her throat. "I just thought. . . Well. . ." She shrugged. "So I came up with this idea. The first forty-five minutes would be Bible study and the rest of the time would be classes in self-improvement."

"Like charm school." No wonder Mavis Parrot had called him.

Daisy nodded. She put up her hand to keep him from interrupting. "With the understanding that any girl who didn't attend Bible study could not participate in the classes."

Jack leaned back against the wall and crossed his arms. "And who, pray tell, teaches these classes? You?"

"No." She glared at him. "Well, not all of them. Lucy Smith, who does my alterations, is giving them sewing lessons; and my hairdresser, Francoise, is styling their hair. She's also instructing them on how to maintain and care for it, and her beautician is working with them on makeup and skin care, and Jillian, who does nails in her salon, is showing the girls how to do manicures and pedicures."

That explained the list of beauty products Mrs. Beemer had mimeographed. Jack snorted. "Oh, yes, I can certainly see the connection between manicures and pedicures and spiritual development."

"I detect a note of sarcasm in your voice, Jack. But I will ignore it."

Obviously, Daisy's confidence had returned. Any other time, Jack might have thought her cute and amusing. This time she aggravated him even more.

She tossed her head back. "And yes, I am teaching. Style and grooming. Manners. Proper grammar. Good grammar is very important, you know."

Frowning, she paused for a moment. "I'm leaving something out. . .elocution. I'm having them read the Bible aloud to improve their elocution. I've found King James wonderful for that."

Jack grunted. "I suppose I should be impressed that the Bible is part of your charm school curriculum."

"It's not a charm school. And I wasn't trying to impress you."

Daisy was beginning to look defensive again.

As she should.

Jack made no effort to hide his cynicism as he took a step toward her. "What about your Ph.D. in hospitality, Daisy? You're leaving that out."

"Au contraire." She glared at him. "We also teach gracious entertaining. Which includes flower arranging and how to set a table and serve properly."

Glancing toward the door, she moved closer, keeping her voice low. "Don't ruin it, Jack. I admit, I may not have been as forthcoming as I should have been, but I wasn't keeping secrets. I just wanted to get the classes up and running before we invited you to see what we were doing."

"That beats all. Now I have to be *invited* into the fellowship hall of my own church."

Daisy's gaze glinted. "I didn't realize it was just *your* church, Jack. I thought it belonged to all of us."

"Don't twist my words, Daisy. You know what I mean. I'm responsible for what goes on here. I have a church board to answer to."

"You still don't get it, Jack!"

Jack glared down at her. "No, Daisy, you don't get it. This is a church, not a finishing school. These are poor girls. Most of them from homes that can barely make ends meet. They are not members of your country club set who need lessons in elocution."

Daisy put her hands on her hips and met him eye-to-eye and toe-to-toe. "Just because they're poor doesn't mean they aren't capable of learning proper manners and how to do things graciously. Take off your blinders, Jack; no one else is going to teach them. Furthermore, when this session is over I intend to take them to museums and concerts and plays. I want my girls to see what's available to them in this world, even if they aren't rolling in money. Give them a vision of possibilities for their lives." She took a deep breath. "I want them to have the knowledge and confidence to use the gifts that God gave them."

Watching Daisy emote, Jack almost forgot how angry he was. In fact, he became quite mesmerized by her blue eyes, flashing with the purity of her commitment; her cheeks, flushed with the fire of her resolve; her voice, ringing with the certainty of her belief.

Her whole petite being quivered with the energy and faith in what she was about.

"In fact, it's all right there in the Bible," she said breathlessly. "You know, that chapter in Romans where it talks about using talents. We studied it last week. Romans twelve. In verse two it says—I made the girls memorize it—'but be ye transformed by the renewing of your mind.' That's what they're doing, transforming their minds, 'that ye may prove what is that good, and acceptable, and perfect, will of God.'"

Daisy straightened. Her expression held a challenge, as if to disagree would be arguing with Him.

"A bit of selective quoting, Daisy?" Jack said mildly. "You left out the first line. 'And be not conformed to this world.'"

He was sorry the instant the words had left his mouth.

Daisy's lips tightened. "You're hopeless."

Before he could respond, the door to the fellowship hall opened behind him.

"There you are, Daisy. Did you find more napkins?"

Jack turned at the sound of the familiar voice.

Daisy's sister-in-law, Rebecca, stood in the threshold.

"Jack. I thought you'd be coaching the boys' basketball."

"Rebecca." He faltered. "What are you doing here?"

She smiled. "I teach the girls cooking and nutrition."

So, Rebecca was in on Daisy's conspiracy, too. Rebecca, whose judgment, wisdom, and compassion, in Jack's mind and heart, were without peer.

He felt as if he'd been hit in the stomach.

"Join us for tea, Jack." Rebecca opened the door wider and stepped aside. "You're in luck. This afternoon I taught the girls to make those scones you're so partial to."

If he wasn't already too weakened to resist, the tempting aroma drifting through the open door along with the teenage chatter was the final assault.

"I'm not sure everyone welcomes me as you do." He glanced at Daisy.

"Of course you're welcome, Jack. After all, it's *your* church." Daisy brushed past him, her chin at a belligerent tilt.

Rebecca took Jack's arm. "This is a real treat. The girls will be thrilled to show off their new skills."

She guided him through the crowded room introducing him to the other teachers, and the young girls crowded around them, whose faces, for the most part, he didn't recognize. And then she drew him to the tea table against the far wall, graced with an elegant handmade lace cloth and resplendent with a sterling silver tea service and a collection of delicate teacups.

Jack recognized them as Daisy's finest.

Rebecca leaned over and whispered, "Nothing's too good for her girls. You know Daisy."

Apparently he didn't—not as well as he'd thought.

A mixed bouquet in an elegant silver tureen sat in the middle of the table. Around it were arranged small compotes of candies and strawberry jam, bowls of nuts, artistic platters of tea sandwiches, homemade cookies, and the aromatic scones Rebecca had promised.

A small round girl with an equally round face leaned toward him. "I arranged the flowers, Pastor Jack."

"Betty, they're lovely." He smiled down at her. "You're lovely."

"I've lost five pounds," she said shyly.

"Well, it shows. Every ounce of it."

"I'm going to lose more," she confided. "Miss Fielding says our bodies are God's temples, and we should take care of them."

It appeared that while Daisy, in her own convoluted way, dealt with improving the vessel, she had not neglected matters of the spirit.

Rebecca put her arm around the girl's shoulders. "We're very proud of Betty. She's becoming our resident expert on nutrition."

Betty beamed.

"Will you please go and tell Mrs. Beemer tea is being served?" Rebecca asked her.

The conspiracy included his own secretary. But then, he'd already guessed that.

Mary Jean, a pretty tomboy of a girl ran up and slapped him on the arm. "Hey, Pastor." She stepped back and posed, one hand on her hip the other behind her head. "What do you think? I made the outfit myself. Well, I had a little help from Mrs. Smith."

Nearby, an older, gray-haired lady, standing behind a girl at the sewing machine, looked up and waved.

Mary Jean's father was head usher and a good friend of Jack's.

"I like that color on you. Has your mother seen your handiwork?" he asked.

"My mom doesn't even know I can sew. I'm going to surprise her."

Jack noticed that several of the girls had similar outfits

but in different colors. "How did you get the material without her knowing?"

"Miss Fielding."

Mary Jean looked fondly across the room at Daisy, who Jack could see was making a pointed effort to stay as far away from him as possible.

"She helped us choose the fabrics that looked best on us. She has such a great sense of style."

"That's true," Jack said.

"Don't tell my dad," Mary Jean said, "but as it turns out, with Miss Fielding leading our classes, I would have come to Bible study even if he hadn't offered my driver's permit as a bribe."

Jack cleared his throat. "How about calling it an incentive?" he suggested.

Mary Jean shrugged. "Whatever."

Rebecca clapped her hands for attention. "Ladies, before we have tea, I'm going to ask Pastor Jack to give a blessing."

Jack wished he'd had more time to prepare. He would have liked to find just the right words to let Daisy know that he was beginning to understand.

"Shall we pray?"

He closed his eyes and heard the familiar rustle and shuffle of feet as the girls bowed their heads.

"Thank You, Lord, for the rich opportunity You have given these girls to grow in knowledge and understanding of Your Word through their study of the Bible.

"Thank You, too, for giving them the opportunity to develop new skills and confidence. We ask Thy blessing,

Lord, on those who teach and those who learn. May all their talents continue to be used, as they are being used now, in ways that glorify Thee.

"Bless this food and the loving hands that prepared it. We ask in Jesus' name. Amen."

The chatter began almost before the amen had died away. He watched as the girls gathered around the elegant table and noted with surprise their restraint. Obviously, they'd been schooled in the proper etiquette: don't elbow in front of others, don't grab, make pleasant conversation.

Truly a transformation from the behavior he was used to at church suppers. He wondered if the change extended to their manners at home.

"If you'll sit down, I'll be happy to serve you, Pastor Jack."

Were his ears deceiving him? Was this the same self-absorbed Meredith who had been a terror in Sunday school since her squalling days in the nursery?

"Cream and sugar?" she asked politely.

"Thank you, Meredith."

He found an empty chair among those lining the side wall.

The girls clustered around him, sipping tea—some even with pinkies extended, which they'd probably learned from the movies. But they couldn't resist devouring the treats with relish. All the while sharing with him praises for their teachers and plans they had for the future.

Meredith, for one, gesturing eloquently with her

newly manicured hands, informed him that she was chairman of the Lou Project. "Do the boys' Bible study and basketball league have a chairman?" She gave him a lidded gaze. "We really should combine efforts with them, don't you think, Pastor Jack?"

It appeared Daisy's plans were coming to fruition.

Rita joined the group a few minutes later when she was replaced at the tea table. She pulled her chair close as she could get to him. In a soft voice, she said, "Miss Fielding had a wonderful idea."

"I'm not surprised."

"She thought we could have a Bible bee."

Jack looked at her, puzzled.

"You know, like a spelling bee. Only instead of spelling words, it's Bible questions."

"Girls against boys," Meredith added.

"Interesting idea," Jack said, calculating how long it would take to get the lads up to speed.

Betty's eyes lit up. "We could combine it with a box social."

Other girls threw in their suggestions, some more inventive than others, but all with one common thread. They each included the boys.

Obviously, Daisy's unique form of proselytizing was working.

He searched the crowded room until he found her.

Their eyes met.

But just as quickly she turned away.

twelve

Daisy had turned from Jack's glance to make a point. If he thought a regretful smile would suffice for all the nasty things he'd said about her enrichment class, not nearly!

She wanted him to grovel.

"Miss Fielding." Betty was at her elbow. "Would it be all right if Mary Jean and Gretchen and I did our Andrews sisters imitation for Pastor Jack? Mrs. Beemer said she'd play the piano for us."

"Of course, Betty. We'd all enjoy that."

A minute later, Mrs. Beemer hit a chord to get everyone's attention.

The three girls snapped their fingers, tapped their toes, and broke into a very credible close harmony of "Boogie Woogie Bugle Boy."

Daisy watched Jack out of the corner of her eye and couldn't help smiling at the way he was getting into the music—grinning, tapping his foot, clapping to the beat.

When the girls were finished, he was the first to call out, "Encore. Encore."

"How about 'Short'nin' Bread,' girls. That's one of your best," Rebecca suggested.

Daisy followed Jack's gaze as he turned toward Rebecca, and she saw his expression alter. So subtly that had she not known him so well. . .loved him so much. . .she would never have discerned it.

The look was deeper than regard. His heart was in his eyes.

Daisy's was suddenly in her throat.

She turned away.

A painful realization began to seep into her spirit.

Mrs. Beemer changed the tempo. Over the random chords she said, "Why don't all you choir members come up here in front. We can end the afternoon with that medley of spirituals you've been rehearsing for Youth Sunday. It'll be good practice."

Daisy studied the grooves in the planked floor, hardly hearing the bustle as the girls assembled, the hum as they found their harmony.

She was thinking back to that lunch at the deli, the day she and Jack had made their wager. The expression in his eyes then, when he spoke of Rebecca.

She realized that the moment Rebecca had stuck her head out the door of the fellowship hall was the moment he began to relent. As if Rebecca's presence was an endorsement.

Daisy had seen his gaze soften then, too, the same as when he'd said Rebecca's name at the deli.

Both times she'd dismissed it.

Now she knew better.

It occurred to her that she had simply not wanted to face the obvious truth. It had been a hopeless cause from the beginning. Plain and simple, she wasn't Jack's type. Never had been.

If Jack harbored unrequited feelings for tall, regal Rebecca, how could anyone expect him to be attracted to little Ditsi Daisy?

She and Rebecca were so different in every way. Rebecca was elegant, refined, practical. Always in control. Never running off at the mouth or after daydreams.

Maybe that's why she and her sister-in-law were so close. They were such complete opposites.

Even though Daisy was choking on this bitter pill of reality, she could never be jealous of her dear "sis."

It wasn't Rebecca's fault that she was so ideal, the loving wife, the perfect mother, and devoted friend.

And how could Daisy blame Jack for having special feelings for Rebecca? The truth was, everybody did. Every woman she knew wanted to emulate her, every man was a little in love with her—and envious of Court.

That clerical collar made Jack no less a man than the rest.

And Rebecca was so modest. She didn't even realize it.

Daisy knew Jack was too honorable to act upon his feelings. But even knowing that, it hurt just as much.

Applause jolted her back into the moment.

The choir had finished before she'd realized they'd even begun.

Jack stood, joining in the enthusiastic applause. When the din died, he said, "I think you girls should give this exact same tea for the church, including the entertainment."

He had been won over. He approved of Daisy's classes.

She tried to swallow the lump in her throat. Tried to feel vindicated. But it didn't matter anymore.

She felt no consolation.

She realized, even if he did grovel, it was too late. Too futile.

She'd been aware that Jack and Rebecca had been good friends before Rebecca married Daisy's brother, Court. Rebecca needed good friends then, newly arrived from the war-torn Philippines to care for a bitter man in a wheelchair.

But she'd had no idea how deep their friendship must have been.

"What do you think, Daisy? Can your girls pull off a tea like this for the congregation?" Jack's smile was gentle and slightly abashed.

"Of course they can," she managed.

His eyes told her he was sorry.

Daisy's heart wrenched. And hardened.

She felt the sting of tears and resolutely blinked them back.

"It's settled then." He turned to Mrs. Beemer. "When we get back to the office we'll decide on a date."

Daisy's childhood fantasies, her years of dreams and yearning, had been dashed in a second by a passing glance.

"Do you have a minute, Daisy?" Jack was beside her again.

"I have to help the girls clean up," she said brusquely.

He would think her still angry. Let him.

It was just as well.

She picked up some used teacups and started toward the kitchen. Jack followed with a stack of dirty plates.

As he put them down on the drain board, he chuckled. "Are my eyes deceiving me? No gloves in sight?" Leaning toward her, he murmured, "Is this my same little girl who is philosophically opposed to ruining her manicure by doing dishes?"

Daisy plunged her hands into the soapy water. Quietly, she replied, "I have to be a good example. And I'm not your little girl." She turned and found herself staring into his laughing brown eyes. "I'm a grown woman. Or hadn't you noticed?"

Jack's gaze turned serious. "Yes," he said, his voice soft enough for only her ears. "Yes, Daisy, I've noticed."

The girls surged around them, bringing dishes, covering the leftover treats with waxed paper, and packing up the china and silver Daisy had brought from home.

Rebecca came into the kitchen and gave Daisy a hug. "It was a great success, honey. I wish I could stay and help clean up, but I have to pick up Davy."

Daisy brushed her cheek with a quick kiss. "You've done more than your share, Becky. Thanks. I'll call you later."

"Aren't you proud of Daisy and the girls, Jack?" Rebecca patted his arm. "Well, see you at the club Saturday."

Daisy flinched. Why did Rebecca have to mention that now?

"What's going on Saturday?"

"Haven't you asked him yet, Daisy?"

"I haven't had a chance."

Rebecca glanced at her watch. "I'm late. Daisy'll give you the details." She waved as she ran out the door. "Great job, girls."

Jack picked up a dish towel. "What's this about Saturday?"

Before Daisy could answer, Meredith interrupted.

"You're not supposed to do that, Pastor Jack." She grabbed the dish towel. "You're our guest."

"Meredith is right," Rita said, carefully sliding teacups into the dishwater. "Miss Fielding says part of entertaining is cleaning up."

Daisy didn't dare look at Jack. She knew for sure what he was thinking. She, who had always had someone else to do the dirty work.

Well, as her grandmother had always said, you have to know how to do things properly in order to tell others.

Jack continued bantering with the girls.

Why was he hanging around?

By the time the dishes were dried and packed, the silver service stored in their special felt bags, and her lace tablecloth and linens folded to take to the cleaners, it was after five.

The girls that were left toted all but three of the boxes out to Daisy's car.

"I'll help Miss Fielding with the rest," Jack said. "She and I have to work out that date for the tea."

Daisy panicked. No way did she want to be alone with him. It had taken all the self-control she could muster not to balk before this.

"I really can't. Not now. I—"

He touched her arm. "It'll only take a minute. Besides, I want to find out what's happening Saturday that you didn't tell me about."

thirteen

Jack squeezed the last box of china into Daisy's trunk. "Who carried these down from your apartment?"

"I did. Watch your fingers." Avoiding his gaze, she reached up and slammed the trunk lid.

"I should follow you home and help unload."

"*No!* No thank you." He was the last person she wanted help from. "If I need any assistance I can call the building super."

Jack leaned against the fender of her little yellow sports car. "You still angry with me, Daisy?"

She shrugged, afraid her voice would give away more than she wanted.

"Come on. Look at your old friend." He reached down and gently lifted her chin.

It was almost six o'clock. The shadows were long and the setting summer sun cast everything in a hazy golden glow.

It had been a hot day, and Jack wasn't wearing a jacket. He loomed above her like some dark, fair-haired movie star. The short-sleeved black clerical shirt strained across his muscled chest and made his broad shoulders seem even broader. An intimidating figure had it not been for his gentle touch and the remorseful smile that played across his lips and in his warm brown eyes.

She turned her head away.

Those eyes got her every time.

"Please forgive me, Daisy. You were right. I should have trusted you. At least given you a chance to explain before I jumped to judgment. Again." He sighed. For a moment he looked thoughtful, then he said, " 'He that trusteth in his own heart is a fool: but whoso walketh wisely, he shall be delivered.' Proverbs 28:26. One of my grandmother's favorites." He looked sheepish. "Sometimes I'm in such a hurry to do what I think is right, I neglect to consider what is wise."

A slight breeze tickled a curl against Daisy's cheek, and Jack reached over to tuck it behind her ear.

She jerked back, burned by the memory of that same gesture the other night in her apartment.

"You *are* still angry."

That isn't it, she wanted to cry out. But to admit the real reason for her reaction would only embarrass them both.

He shoved his hands into his pockets. "I can't say I blame you. I guess I was pretty hard on you this afternoon."

"You were." The top of the car was down, and Daisy slung her purse across into the passenger's seat. "But it was my own fault." She opened the car door. "I was sure you'd think the classes frivolous, but I figured once you saw them you'd be convinced—"

"Which I was."

It was an awkward moment, but he'd had the courage to confess, so should she. "I'm ashamed to admit it, but

I knew you'd have to get approval from your board. I figured they'd *really* think the classes were trivial, and even if you were finally able to convince them otherwise, by that time summer would be nearly over, and it would be too late to do anything."

Jack laughed. "You were probably right."

"I still should have leveled with you."

"Maybe." He smiled. "But your intentions were pure." He hoisted himself off the fender, and Daisy spilled into the car as if she'd been shot.

Before she could pull the door closed he was standing there, holding on to the handle.

"Before you take off, there is one more thing. What about Saturday? Or is that another of your well-kept secrets that I'm not supposed to know about?"

"Rebecca wouldn't have mentioned it if it were a secret."

Jack shut the door and leaned forward, crossing his arms on the rolled-down window.

His face was decidedly too close for comfort.

She pushed the key into the ignition. "I had a contractor go over Lou's property to see what it will cost to make the necessary repairs." As she straightened, she inched farther away in the seat. "Excluding the painting. I figure I can get the kids to do that. . . . What are you grinning about, Jack?"

He tweaked her nose. "Now you're a paint contractor."

She slapped his hand away, trying to appear indifferent while her heart raced at his nonchalant touch of affection.

"It's going to cost a lot," she said, struggling for equanimity. "The house needs a new roof. And we're going to have to build her a ramp. The garden fence is falling down."

"How's the inside?"

"You haven't seen it?"

"Not yet. Didn't think I needed to with you in charge."

"So now you have confidence in me. It's about time," she tried to joke.

"I hope you've remembered to pick up the mail?"

"Of course. I said I would, didn't I? And making the bank deposits, and taking the bills and receipts to my accountant, and—"

"Enough. I get the picture. I'm proud of you, Daisy, but this all started when we were talking about Saturday."

"I'm getting to that. So, I had my secretary call—"

"I didn't know you had a secretary."

"Part-time. Anyway, I had her call a group of my friends from the country club, and we're going to have a party Saturday night to raise the money we need to fix up Lou's property."

Jack stood up. "That's terrific, Daisy."

"And they don't even know Lou," Daisy pointed out. "Which goes to prove what I've always told you, Jack. Folks can be rich and still be compassionate."

"I never said—"

"Not outright. But that's what you've always inferred, and you know it. 'The poor shall inherit the earth,' isn't necessarily referring to the financially poor, you know." Her tone had become belligerent.

"Actually its the meek that inherit the earth," he said, mildly. "According to Matthew 5, the poor inherit the Kingdom of heaven."

"Whatever. You know what I mean."

"Are you trying to pick a fight, Daisy?"

"Yes. No—I've got to go." Daisy put her left foot on the brake and pumped the accelerator. The engine coughed and caught. "I thought you might like to fill out my table Saturday. There'll be eight of us. Naturally, you'll be my guest."

"I'd like that, Daisy."

"Don't worry, it's not like a date. Since I'm chairman, I'll have to circulate. I don't want to be with someone I need to worry about and impress."

Jack looked amused. "I'm your guy."

As she backed out of the parking space, he called, "What time am I supposed to be there?"

"Seven o'clock. It's dressy sport." She wheeled the car toward the exit. "But I guess that doesn't affect you."

That didn't sound very gracious, she thought, spinning onto Third Street. But so what?

fourteen

Saturday night, Jack stood in the threshold of the country club lounge, scanning the crowded room for his "non-date," Daisy.

He hadn't felt particularly complimented when she made such a point about wanting to be with someone she didn't have to impress or worry about. It certainly put him in his place. But he was probably getting his just desserts. If Jack looked on Court as a brother, then little tagalong Daisy had been cast in the role of pesky, annoying, but lovable little sister, to be tolerated and teased.

The room was packed with women dressed in simple, understated elegance Daisy had called dressy sport, manicured, pedicured—he was sure—and bejeweled, and tanned men in tailored sport jackets and expensive ties.

Daisy accused him of being a reverse snob. It was hard not to be when he saw such need on one hand and such opulence on the other. Just one of those diamond bracelets could build a much needed youth center in his neighborhood.

"Judge not, that ye be not judged," rang in his ears. Daisy would remind him that many important causes were supported by some of the very people in this room.

He tended to be more skeptical.

Still, tonight they had gathered to help an old woman they didn't know. Perhaps it was time he reassessed.

The meld of voices, laughter, and the clink of glasses had reached a high pitch, subdued only by the rich silk drapes and thick Oriental rug on the lounge floor. Two chandeliers, equidistant from the center, splashed the teak walls with fractured rainbows.

Though Daisy was tiny, from his six-foot-four-inch advantage, Jack spotted her without too much trouble. All he had to do was look for a circle of smiling faces, and she'd be in the center. In her flowered pink dress, she looked as if she were wrapped in rose petals.

He liked watching her in action. She was so full of animation and joy, her golden curls danced as she spoke.

Now she was focusing on a tall, dark-haired man who appeared to be about Jack's age. His grim mouth cracked into a smile.

She was irresistible.

For an instant, Jack felt an intense dislike for the guy.

At that moment, Daisy caught sight of him and waved him over. "I'm glad you're here. Have you met Greg Johnson?"

"I don't think so." Jack clasped the man's extended hand. "But your name is familiar."

"It should be. Greg's the contractor on the new city hall. Greg, Pastor Jack McCutcheon, my spiritual advisor." She made a face at Jack.

It appeared at least some of her ire had dissipated.

"Well, Jack, what do you think of the crowd?" she asked.

"Amazing. How many people do you suppose are here?"

"What would you say, Greg? Sixty-five, seventy?"

"At least."

"At a contribution of twenty dollars a person, not bad." Daisy gave Jack a what-do-you-have-to-say-about-that look. "I think this evening will cover just about all the costs to repair Lou's house."

Greg looked down at Daisy with a much too admiring gaze. "It's amazing what this girl can accomplish with a few phone calls."

"Isn't it," Jack said.

Daisy pursed her lips. "Jack knows all my secrets. My secretary made most of the calls," she confessed. "But I called you, didn't I, Greg? And I didn't have to twist your arm, either."

"I wouldn't have minded if you had. Your arm-twisting is good therapy, Daisy."

The man was flirting with her.

Who could blame him?

"I'll remember that, Greg." She gave him a twinkling smile.

Daisy was flirting with him.

Well, why shouldn't she? After all, Jack wasn't her date. She had made that abundantly clear. Still, she did seem a bit obvious, the way she was leading the guy on with that smile of hers. And he didn't take much leading.

Dinner was announced, and Daisy linked her arms through theirs. "Greg is involved in a good cause of his own," she said as they moved with the crowd toward the dining room.

"I wouldn't say that too loudly. My cause is not particularly popular in these circles."

"Well, I think the members of your organization are not only compassionate but courageous," Daisy said staunchly. "Greg volunteers in the reparation project for Japanese internees, helping them get back property that was illegally confiscated during the war."

"Good for you," Jack said.

Greg gave him a sardonic smile. "I appreciate your endorsement. You're definitely in the minority, considering the prevailing prejudice against the Japanese."

As they entered the dining room, their conversation was interrupted by the bustle and confusion of folks searching for their tables and from the music of a combo in the corner. The room shimmered in the soft light of overhanging crystal chandeliers and votive candles at each setting. A loose arrangement of deep pink bougainvillea occupied the center of the round tables covered with pink cloths.

Jack looked over at Greg. "Can you guess what Daisy's favorite color is?"

"Could it be pink?"

"You've got it."

"You can tease me all you want, but I don't believe in expensive floral decorations for a fund-raiser. The bougainvillea grows wild in the lot next to Lou's house," Daisy told Greg. "The girls from our Bible study group at church did the centerpieces."

"Remind me to compliment them," Jack said, smiling down at her.

Daisy had arranged place cards at their table, so Jack sat on her left, Greg on her right.

Was she trying to make him jealous or Greg?

The rest of the table was already seated. The men stood as Daisy made the introductions: "Tom Smith, our city councilman, and his wife, Jessica." Everyone already knew Court and Rebecca. It seemed Greg did have a dinner partner of his own, his sister, Mary.

No wonder the man felt so free to flirt with Daisy.

But he seemed like a good person. If Greg was Daisy's choice, Jack would have to get better acquainted to decide if he was suitable for her.

When everyone was finally seated, the musicians gave a flourish, and Daisy stepped up to the microphone.

She asked everyone to please rise and invited Jack to give the invocation.

Jack needed no microphone. His voice carried to the farthest corners of the room as he prayed for Lou's healing, thanking God for the friends who had gathered to help her, asking His blessing on those of such generous heart and the food that sustained them.

Daisy's welcome was brief. She told a bit about Lou and why she was so deserving, then concluded, "You'll all be happy to know that an anonymous donor has underwritten this party so all the money you've contributed goes directly into the Lou Green Fund."

While everyone applauded, Court leaned over to Jack. "Guess who the anonymous donor is?"

"You?"

"My sister. It's only me if she runs short."

Rebecca poked him on the arm. "You weren't supposed to say anything. What do you think anonymous means?"

"Don't worry, we'll never tell," Greg said.

His sister, Mary, shook her head. "Typical Daisy."

The councilman's wife agreed. "I love having Daisy on my committee. She never submits a bill."

"People have been saying nice things about you, Daisy," the councilman said when she returned. Greg rose along with Jack to seat her.

Jack won. "Good job, Daisy," he said, pushing in her chair. "You were short, sweet, and you got off the stage."

"Thank you," she said pleasantly. "Kind words from a professional and *always* my most severe critic."

Well, maybe she still was a bit piqued with him.

Court grinned from across the table.

He could have been more effusive in his compliment, he supposed. With anyone else he would have been. But this was Daisy, after all. As she'd said, someone he didn't have to "worry about or impress."

He didn't know why that continued to irritate him.

It turned out Daisy didn't have to circulate, as she'd expected. All during dinner people swarmed around their table like bees to a blossom.

Jack sat back and watched her with awe. It was amazing how she managed to remember every name and in her introductions had something nice to say about each person. Not a soul left the table without feeling special.

"Jack, I want you to meet Ruth Pollard. Ruth is doing a fantastic job as area chairman of the Jimmy Fund."

The councilman's wife, Jessica, leaned forward. "Wasn't that the twelve-year-old cancer patient Ralph Edwards interviewed?"

Ruth nodded.

There was Bill Gray who was on the board of the YMCA; and Ann Jason, president of the Junior League, who had "initiated some wonderful new policies"; and Lisa Jones who was chairman of the upcoming Red Cross fund-raising ball. . . "With Lisa in charge it's bound to be a success."

As the waiters began pouring coffee, Daisy tilted her head toward Jack and whispered, "Perhaps you'd like to revise your global prejudice about the country club set?"

Before he had a chance to reply, the music segued from dinner to dance. Daisy, Mary, and Jessica jumped up to go "powder their noses." Court asked Rebecca to dance, leaving Tom, the councilman; Greg; and Jack at the table.

Tom polished off the last bite of his baked Alaska and wiped his mouth with his napkin. He was a small, dapper man with a blond, well-trimmed mustache. "Which hospital is your friend, Lou, in?" he asked Jack.

"Fairhaven."

"That's one of Sherm Locksley's convalescent hospitals," Tom said. "He owns a string of them, you know."

"I didn't," Greg said.

"And some less desirable properties. I think he's here tonight." Tom scanned the room. "Don't see him now.

Maybe he left early."

"I've never met him," Jack said. "Was his father Herbert Locksley?"

Tom nodded.

"Wonderful man. Died a few years ago. Member of our church."

Greg moved over and took Daisy's vacated chair. "Where is your church, Jack?"

"On the corner of York and Third."

"That's a coincidence. Sherm recently offered me a project in your area. Wants to raze a couple of old buildings and build a bar."

Jack frowned. "That's all we need, another bar in the neighborhood. It's bad enough that the children have to pass three on their way to the elementary school."

"I turned it down," Greg said. "Fortunately, I'm in a position to choose my projects. And even if I weren't, I don't build bars."

"Do you remember the address?" Jack pushed back his coffee cup.

"Somewhere in the one hundred block. One hundred one. Yes, that's it. One hundred and one, Third Street."

"That's right next door to the *church*." Jack felt a deep surge of anger.

Then shock.

"That's the address of Lou's Lube!"

fifteen

"The buildings Sherm's planning to tear down are Lou's Lube?" Greg said.

"How can he do that?" Jack asked, enraged.

"I wouldn't put anything past him," Tom said and frowned. "I've heard he checks out the background of the elderly patients in his convalescent hospitals and uses the information to his advantage."

"If he's already making plans to tear down the garage with Lou still in the hospital, he must know something," Greg said.

Jack glanced up and saw the three women returning. "Let's keep this to ourselves. At least for tonight. After all Daisy's work, I'd hate to ruin the party for her. I'll tell her tomorrow."

"Mum's the word," Greg said, vacating Daisy's chair.

Tom muttered to Jack under his breath. "I'll do some sleuthing at city hall. See if Sherm's applied for any permits lately."

"I'd appreciate that."

Daisy danced around behind Jack and dropped her clutch purse into her chair. "You all look so serious. I think we need to trip the light fantastic, don't you, Greg?"

If that wasn't an obvious slight at Jack, he didn't know

what was. Well, two could play that game.

Jack smiled at Daisy. "Good thinking. Mary, may I have this dance?"

Dancing with Greg's sister was not disagreeable in the least. In fact, she was a very attractive young woman.

But she wasn't Daisy.

For the rest of the evening, Jack did his duty as an amiable guest, made small talk, and danced with all the ladies at the table. Except Daisy, who always managed to be out of reach, too busy flirting with Greg and flitting about the room spreading charm as naturally as a hummingbird spreads pollen.

Suddenly the music stopped. There was another flourish from the band, and once again Daisy stepped up to the microphone, this time to announce that an anonymous donor had purchased weekly car washes and routine servicing for a year from Lou's Lube, to be auctioned off.

Jack caught Court's eye, and they both laughed.

He looked around him. The room was beautiful, the people were beautiful, and everyone was having a beautiful time. Daisy had done a great job. Her benefit was an obvious success, to say nothing of the money she'd raised for Lou.

The evening was beginning to wind down when Rebecca gave him a kiss on the cheek. "Pumpkin time for those of us with kiddies."

Court came up behind his wife. "See you tomorrow in church."

Tom and Jessica followed them out, complaining

about their own baby-sitter issues.

Greg's sister moved over and sat down beside Jack. "I've really enjoyed meeting you."

He could see an invitation in her eyes.

She was a lovely woman, just the right age, and very bright. But somehow, he just wasn't interested.

"I enjoyed talking to you, too, Mary."

"It's been a lovely evening."

"It has indeed."

"Daisy makes everything look so easy," Mary said.

She was forcing conversation. Hoping they might make a connection. At his age, he knew the signs.

"It takes a lot of planning and hard work for it to look that way," she continued. "I know. I've done a lot of these parties myself."

Greg joined them. "Daisy's an amazing woman, all right." His admiring gaze followed her across the room.

Jack was suddenly conscious of how often he had taken the "amazing Daisy" for granted.

"Greg's always had a crush on Daisy," Mary confided.

"Who hasn't?" Greg chuckled.

The man had just echoed Jack's thoughts.

"The thing about Daisy is, the men love her and so do the women," Mary said. "None of us are jealous of her, she's so genuinely sweet."

"She's always been that way," Jack mused absently, struck with the fact it was the truth.

The crowd was beginning to thin, and it wasn't long before Greg and Mary prepared to leave, also. Over Mary's objections.

"Next time you can bring your own car," Greg said to his sister.

"Brothers." Mary shook her head and extended her hand to Jack. Her brown eyes were warm. "I hope we see each other again."

"I'm sure we will."

Nice folks, but Jack was not sorry to see them go.

At the empty table, Jack mused on why such a suitable woman did not attract him. He found himself watching Daisy circulate among the remaining guests, watching her dance.

It seemed that every man in the room wanted one final dance with the lady in pink.

She hadn't even looked his direction in the last half hour. He could have left with Greg and Mary, for all she would have noticed.

It irritated him. It surprised him how much. Under normal circumstances he would have just left. Taught her a lesson—if she cared.

When she finally did glance his way, it seemed almost accidental. It was a quick, indifferent look over the shoulder of a young man with whom she was about to dance—for the third time.

But who was counting?

Jack had had it with this game.

He got up and strode across the dance floor. Not at all the way a minister should. There was fire in his belly, and he knew, in his eye.

"Excuse me," he said, struggling not to take his ire out on the young fellow. After all, it wasn't his fault.

"Would you mind if I had this dance with Daisy? They're playing our song."

Before either he or Daisy could respond, Jack swung her out and twirled her across the dance floor.

He could see she was angry.

He'd gotten her attention. Finally.

"Really, Jack. 'Won't You Come Home, Bill Bailey' our song?"

Daisy tried to pull away, but he wasn't about to let her. She needed a lesson.

"You interrupted my conversation with a very interesting young man."

"*Young* is right."

"He's exactly my age." Daisy glared up at him. "What do you think, I need a father figure like you who's ten years older?"

"I didn't say that."

"You really are a dog in the manger, you know. You're not interested in me, yourself, but you're irritated when someone else is."

"That's not so." He swung her out, twirled her twice and drew her back. "It's just, I think you need someone more grounded, more mature, that's all."

She leaned back in his arms. "Like Greg?"

"Maybe so. Maybe like Greg."

"I must say, you didn't look all that pleased when I was dancing with him, either."

"Reading my mind again, Daisy? Or just wishful thinking? It's obvious you're still trying to punish me." He slowed his tempo to halftime, and dipped her back, his face close to hers. "Frankly, I think I've used admirable restraint considering the way you've ignored me all evening."

"I warned you."

"There's a limit."

"I wouldn't have thought you cared enough to notice."

Abruptly, he pulled her upright and stopped dancing, right in the middle of the dance floor.

"Okay, Daisy, how about a truce? You stop this little game of yours, and I'll start noticing."

"Dance, Jack. Everybody's looking," Daisy muttered beneath her breath.

"Only if you promise."

"I promise."

"Okay, then." He drew her back into his arms and twirled her in a showy circle around the floor. When the music slowed to a foxtrot, so did they, step for step, spin for spin, dip for dip, in perfect harmony.

Well, why not? He'd taught her everything she knew.

"One thing I will say for you, Jack—"

"What's that?" he murmured, resting his chin against her hair.

"For a minister—I take that back—for just about anybody, you're the best dancer I know."

He felt like saying, *Then why didn't you want to dance with me?* Instead, he pulled her closer. But not unseemly so.

"Remember when I was little and I'd put my feet on top of yours, and you'd dance with me that way?"

"Uh-huh."

She smelled so fresh and good. Like blooming lilacs.

Daisy tilted her head back. "Do you remember how you and Court—you really, Court's never been a very good dancer—how you gave me a dance lesson before my first prom?"

Jack chuckled. "That callow youth was way too young for you, too."

The music had turned slow and sweet. Under his breath, Jack absently hummed along. *You made me love you, I didn't want to do it.* . .and felt her head relax against his heart.

sixteen

The following morning, Daisy sat in a pew near the back of the church, vaguely aware of the medley of hymns Mrs. Beemer was playing. As she stared at the Sunday bulletin, her thoughts drifted back to the benefit the night before. Mostly the last thrilling but confusing hour.

She and Jack had danced until the combo packed up their instruments.

He had walked her to her car. She remembered his arm lightly around her shoulders and the shiver that ran through her, even though the gesture seemed less intimate than friendly.

She remembered the night sounds of crickets and katydids, and the stars and the sweet scent of night-blooming jasmine.

She'd felt suddenly shy when they reached the car, anticipating what might come next. Her heart accelerated as he leaned down. . .and deposited a quick, brotherly kiss on her cheek.

"Thanks for inviting me, Daisy. You gave a beautiful party." He helped her into the car like the perfect gentleman he always was and slammed the door. With a grin, he gave the admonition he'd given her since she'd gotten her driver's license, "Lock your door, Ditsi."

It was like a splash of cold water.

Yet on the dance floor she had sensed a difference. Or had she just imagined that he'd held her closer as they danced?

Had she dreamed she'd felt his heart beating against her cheek?

Mrs. Beemer segued into "May Jesus Christ Be Praised," reminding Daisy that she was in church to think about Jesus, not Jack.

The congregation stood and the choir, in their royal blue robes, filed in. Jack followed, a head taller than the two deacons who flanked him.

Just the sight of him made Daisy's heart leap. She couldn't help it. He was so handsome and strong, and virtuous.

She sighed. So very virtuous. Not even a proper kiss.

The black robe hung from his broad shoulders, and he moved with easy grace. He looked fit and tan and dignified, except for that shock of sun-bleached hair that refused to be controlled.

A brief invocation, announcements made, offering taken, the doxology sung—"Praise God from Whom All Blessings Flow"—and then Jack's sermon.

He rose and stepped to the pulpit. Bowing his head, he began, as always, "Let the words of my mouth, and the meditations of our hearts, be acceptable in Thy sight, O Lord, our strength, and our redeemer. Amen."

She trembled at the sound of his deep sonorous voice. His preaching voice. It was so compelling.

"Amen," the congregation echoed.

His sermon was on forgiveness. A universal message,

but as it progressed, Daisy felt as if he had written it just for them.

Oh, if it were only so.

". . .As we forgive, we are creating an atmosphere of love for ourselves and others. We want our family and friends to know we value them and our relationship. . . ."

Had his gaze touched her as he scanned through the congregation?

He continued. "Forgiveness provides a way around differences and disagreements that both we and those we care about might never be able to accomplish."

Yes. This time she could feel his intentions. She was sure of it. She was.

Oh, please, dear God, make it so.

"May we all allow God's love to move through our words of forgiveness to unite us in our minds and in our hearts."

He quoted Luke 6:37. " 'Judge not, and ye shall not be judged: condemn not, and ye shall not be condemned' "— he paused—" 'forgive, and ye shall be forgiven.' "

After a moment of prayerful silence, he returned to his chair, the choir sang, and then the congregation rose for the benediction, joining together in the final hymn, "Teach Me Thy Way, O Lord."

Jack strode down the center aisle toward her, and Daisy's heart beat faster as she willed him to look in her direction and was rewarded.

Even though she recognized it as the smile that blessed them all, it fed the flames of love that burned in her heart.

After the service, Daisy waited on a bench in the narthex for Jack to finish greeting the parishioners. They would be taking the altar flowers to Lou, as they had each Sunday since her accident.

She watched him shaking hands, looking each person in the eye with an encouraging word or a pat on the arm; bend to give special attention to a stooped old lady in a flowered hat; admire a little boy's toy; tease a group of teenage girls.

As she continued to wait, she reflected on his sermon. *Forgiveness, be it of ourselves or others, lifts a heavy burden,* she thought. *It gives an opportunity for a fresh start.*

Maybe that was one of the things he was getting at.

She was Jack's good friend, and she knew she always would be. His "little sister." He still sometimes introduced her that way.

If that wasn't sending a message, she couldn't imagine what would.

She had to be honest with herself. Nothing he'd said or done last night or even before, no matter how much she'd hoped, had led her to believe otherwise.

It was time she accept that.

When this Lou thing was finished and summer was over, maybe she'd move to New York. She might even get a job. She'd be twenty-five on her next birthday. She had to think of her future.

A future that didn't include Pastor Jack McCutcheon.

Lost in her thoughts, it took a moment to notice the surrounding silence and the dark figure standing in front of her.

Jack's voice brought her to attention. "It'll just take me a couple of minutes to get out of my robe, and I'll be with you."

"I'll get the flowers from the altar and meet you in the car," she said.

"Yours or mine?"

"Yours. I have the top down. Last week they got blown all over the place, remember?"

"Afterward I'll take you to lunch," he said.

"Let me—"

"Daisy. . ." He gave her a warning look. "It may not be as fancy, but it's my turn."

"Turn, shmurn, what does it matter between friends?"

"Precisely," he said, turning. His black robe billowed out behind him as he strode back down the center aisle.

For the time being, Daisy became too engaged in the present to continue pondering her future. Especially when on the way to the convalescent hospital, Jack told her what he had learned about the possible jeopardy of Lou's Lube.

"Sherm Locksley? He was at the benefit last night." Daisy was so angry she felt about to explode.

"Take it easy," Jack warned. "We don't know all the facts yet. Your friend, the councilman, said he'd look into it and get back to me."

"I wonder what it could be? I've been scrupulous about paying her bills," Daisy said.

"Those you know about."

"You're right. I should have thought of that. You know how some old folks tend to stash things away and forget about them."

"You don't have to be old to have that problem," Jack said, his tone rueful.

"I hate to worry the old dear if we don't have to," Daisy said. "Maybe after our visit we can go by and check her house."

"You might ask her if there was additional mail she'd put someplace that you could have missed." Jack swung a right into the parking lot of Fairhaven Convalescent Hospital. "At least then we'd have a place to start."

After Lou had exclaimed over the church flowers and opened the box of chocolates Daisy had brought, Daisy broached the subject of mail she might have missed.

Sure enough, Lou admitted that sometimes, when she was in a hurry, she shoved things into the bottom drawer of her desk. "But you don't have to worry about my house payments," she said. "The bank extended my loan. The guy told me to ignore 'em. The bills were just a formality."

Daisy exchanged a worried glance with Jack.

"Do you remember the man's name?"

"Nope. Just some man from the bank."

Daisy and Jack went directly from the convalescent hospital to Lou's house.

Scanning the cluttered living room, Jack said, "Hope we find what we're looking for in the desk. I wouldn't know where to start, otherwise." He reached down and petted one of Lou's purring calicos that had wrapped itself around his leg.

"It's in here," Daisy said, entering the front bedroom.

The bottom drawer of the desk was so packed it was difficult to open. Pulling it all the way out, Daisy dumped the contents on the bed. Then she and Jack began the task of sorting through the newspaper clippings, advertisements and magazine subscriptions, charitable requests, and brochures. As the pile thinned, Daisy began to lose hope.

"What's this?" Jack picked up an envelope near the bottom of the stack that had the logo of a local bank in the corner of the envelope. He tore it open and quickly scanned the contents.

Daisy's throat tightened. She could see by the expression on his face that it was something horrendous. "What is it?"

Silently, he handed her the letter. "Read the second paragraph."

"Because of your default in making payment, notwithstanding notice of foreclosure, the foreclosure sale of your property will be conducted on Monday, August 4, 1948, at 9:00 a.m., on the courthouse steps. . . ."

Daisy stared at the sheet of paper clutched in her trembling hand. "That's tomorrow morning."

seventeen

Jack leaned over Daisy's shoulder. "Look at that." He pointed to the letterhead. "Sherman Locksley is listed as a member of the board of directors."

"No wonder he has such easy access to the patients' information. I'll bet you anything he was the one who told Lou to ignore her loan payments." Fresh rage roiled within Daisy. "Isn't there some way we can stop him?"

"As long as it can't be proved that he's the one who told her, he's not doing anything illegal."

"Just immoral, taking advantage of the old and the infirm."

"That's the rumor. Maybe we'll know more when we hear from Tom."

"After the fact. What good will it do when the property has already been auctioned? Besides, I don't need any more proof of Sherm's duplicity. He approached Greg with the plans to build a bar on this location. Right here where we're standing. That and his connection to the bank should be enough to convince anyone." Daisy frowned. "Don't they have any zoning restrictions?"

"In this neighborhood?" Jack rolled his eyes. "Hardly. It's zoned for commercial, so he can build anything he wants."

"You should love that. A bar sharing your parking lot.

Sin on Saturday night and only a short walk to repentance Sunday."

"You found the silver lining," Jack said dryly.

"Oh, Jack, it's so terribly sad." Daisy blinked back tears. "Lou and Harry lived in this house from the time they were first married. It's filled with loving memories. Obviously, she doesn't have any money. Where will she go? Some old people's home where they don't allow cats? What will happen to Betty and Boots?"

"Rick will probably take them."

"And what about Rick? There's not a great demand for one-handed mechanics, you know. It's just awful." Tears blinding her, she wiped her eyes with the back of her fist. "And even if Lou gets on her feet, the most she'll be able to do is supervise. She'll never be able to work on the cars again. Which is what she loves to do most."

Daisy gave a little catching sob. "The accident didn't do her in, but I'm just afraid this might. Old people can die of a broken heart, you know."

One of Lou's cats jumped into Daisy's lap. Absently she stroked it. "The party was such a big success, and we made all that money to fix up the property, and there'll be no property to fix. Poor Lou."

Jack put his hand over hers. "Don't worry, we'll see that Lou's taken care of."

Usually, Daisy would have luxuriated in his touch, but not now. She hardly noticed.

"What's the matter with us?" She jumped to her feet. The cat slipped to the floor with a cantankerous mew.

"We're talking as if Sherm's bar is ready to open up

for business. It's not over 'til it's over, Jack. And I'm not ready to give up until it is. The good Lord didn't give us brains to sit on them. He gave us brains so we could help Him out."

Jack smiled at her.

"What's so funny?"

"You are. Funny and gentle and sweet. And about as kind and compassionate a person as I've ever known. And certainly the most spirited." He drew her into his arms. Patting her on the shoulder, he said, "I just want you to know. You're not alone in this." He leaned back and looked deeply into her eyes. "God is on our side."

Over before it had begun. Those were hardly the words she was waiting for.

"Oh, please." Daisy pulled away. "We can't expect God to solve every problem that we create. Lou allowed this to happen, for whatever reasons. It's up to us to work it out."

"With that logic, then it's up to Lou. Not you or me." Jack folded his arms. "Just as Lou can depend on you, even more, we can depend on Him, if not to solve the problem, at the very least to give guidance and counsel. But we have to be willing to listen. Remember the twenty-fourth verse of Psalm seventy-three?"

"Can't say as I do."

" 'Thou shalt guide me with thy counsel, and afterward receive me to glory.' "

Daisy tilted her head and gave him an assessing look. "In this world, or the next?"

"Both."

They stared silently at each other. She broke the spell. "You're pretty good at remembering those gems."

He smiled. "Maybe because I've had to remind myself so often." He glanced down at his watch. "It's two o'clock. We'll think more clearly if we have something to eat."

As Jack began stuffing the papers back into the drawer, Daisy neatly folded the bank's letter and slid it back in its envelope, then tucked it into her purse.

Checking on the cats' food and water on their way out, she was encouraged to see that Rick was keeping his end of the bargain.

As they walked down Lou's front steps, Daisy was overwhelmed with a great sense of urgency. "I'm really not hungry. I think I'd choke if I tried to eat anything. May I have a rain check on lunch?"

"Of course."

"I need to go home. Make some phone calls."

eighteen

Jack was waiting on the curb when Daisy's yellow car squealed to a stop in front of him. They had twenty minutes to get to the courthouse. It was going to be a tight race.

"Sorry I'm late. I was waiting for a phone call from Daniel." The instant he slammed the door, Daisy took off. She glanced over. "You know my attorney, Daniel Essex?"

Jack nodded.

"He's going to look into some possibilities for us. I was hoping he'd get back to me before I had to leave."

Her cheeks were pink from the wind, her blond curls whipping about her face.

"You look calmer than I expected," Jack said.

Daisy shrugged. "I've done what I can." She smiled at him. "To quote my favorite cleric, now it's in God's hands."

They pulled into the parking lot with five minutes to spare and hurried up the street to the courthouse. Ten or twelve people already milled around at the bottom of the steps.

"Real estate brokers," Jack surmised.

"I wonder if that louse, Sherm, will show up." Daisy said. "He'll probably send someone else from the bank to do his dirty work."

The air was muggy, with no breeze. Even at nine o'clock it was hotter than usual for an August morning.

"It's the humidity." Jack yanked at his clerical collar with his index finger.

"Hey, aren't you gonna say hello?" a voice boomed behind them.

Daisy whirled around.

Sherm Locksley was standing on the strip of lawn between the sidewalk and the street, grinning at her from under the shade of a ficus tree. "This is an embarrassment of riches, Daisy, seeing you twice in two days."

Jack could foresee trouble. "Let him be," he murmured, grasping Daisy's hand.

She pulled free. "Embarrassment is right!" she said, striding over to the man who now viewed her with some surprise.

"It's an embarrassment even to know you, Sherman Locksley, after what you did to Lou."

Jack called, "Come on, Daisy, it won't do any good."

But Daisy wasn't listening. Hands on her hips, she glared up at Sherm. "You're a real Judas, you know."

"Whoa. What are you talking about?" Sherm crossed his arms and looked down at her, the smile frozen on his lips, his gray eyes icy.

"You know very well what I'm talking about. You told Lou that her loan payment had been extended and not to bother opening the letters from the bank. A formality. Ha!"

Daisy was so angry she shook, and for a moment Jack

was afraid she would haul off and hit the guy.

"How stupid do you think I am?" Sherm said. "That would be illegal."

"So, you admit it." Her voice had risen to a pitch that was attracting attention.

"I don't admit anything." Sherm wasn't smiling now. "If you're going to make that kind of accusation, you better prove it with the paper it's written on."

"You know there's no paper, you lowlife."

Jack walked over and placed a restraining hand on her shoulder. "Come on, Daisy."

She wouldn't budge.

Sherm shoved his hands into his pockets. "I don't know what the old lady—"

"You mean *Lou Green*!" Daisy spat.

"You know how old folks get confused. Imagine things."

"Not Lou," Daisy said.

"Come on, Daisy, they're starting the auction." Jack pulled her toward the group of people bunched around a man at the foot of the courthouse steps. Over his shoulder he muttered, "I'm glad your father isn't here to see this, Sherm."

Jack kept a calming arm around Daisy during the disposal of the first two properties. When Lou's came up for bid, only a few people remained.

The auctioneer flipped to the third sheet of paper and read, "This is the time and place specified in notices previously given for the foreclosure sale of the property located at one zero one, Third Street. The bank has bid the amount of its deed of trust that, including interest, is the sum of $1,452.00. Do I hear any further bidding?"

"One thousand seven hundred fifty."

"Daniel!" Daisy turned and threw her arms around the man who had come up beside them. "You arrived just in time!"

Daniel Essex was not quite as tall as Jack; had dark hair; dark, brooding eyes; and a rather somber expression. But he managed to wrench out a smile for Daisy.

Jack had met Daniel casually at a couple of big parties at Court and Rebecca's. Although the man had always been genial, Jack and he had never really gotten acquainted.

The two shook hands.

"You're a welcome sight," Jack said.

"Two thousand." Sherm stalked over. He had obviously expected the property to go at the bank's bid, and his anger was palpable. "I see you got your loser lawyer involved."

Daniel smiled benignly. "Two thousand and three hundred."

When the bidding reached three thousand dollars, Sherm stomped off, muttering, "It's not worth it."

Daisy returned his bruising glare with a disdainful smile.

"It may not be worth it to him, but it sure is to us." She beamed at the men on either side of her. "This means Lou will be able to keep her house, and the church won't have a tavern next door."

"You seem pretty confident. So, who's your client,

Daniel?" Jack glanced pointedly at Daisy.

"Don't look at me," she said, her expression innocent.

"It's a consortium of charitable givers who prefer to remain anonymous." Daniel swung his briefcase from his right hand to his left. "They keep some assets liquid for situations such as this."

"How do we know this secret consortium intends to return the property to Lou?" Jack said.

"It's a bit more complicated than that," Daniel said.

"Tell me."

Daisy suggested, "Why don't we talk about this over brunch at the club—when Daniel has finished tying up all the legal aspects?"

"What's the game, Daisy?" Jack was becoming annoyed. "If you can't let me in on the secret, what am I doing here?"

Daisy's gaze followed Daniel's receding silhouette as he ran up the steps and disappeared into the courthouse.

"You'll just have to trust me," she murmured.

nineteen

The master manipulator. Daisy was doing it again.

Jack struggled to control his temper. He took a deep breath. He could tell by the expression on her face she wasn't about to budge.

He might as well relax. She'd tell him in due time. She always did.

As they walked toward the car, he said, "I don't think I've ever seen you act the way you did with Sherm Locksley."

"I admit, it wasn't my grandest moment. But even Jesus had His limit with the money changers in the temple."

"I suppose we can find a parallel here," Jack admitted, "but I don't recall Jesus resorting to name-calling."

Daisy refused to be contrite. She tossed her curls. "I'm sure they had their own vernacular in those days." She looked at him through narrowed eyes. "I don't need a sermon, Jack."

"Who, me?" He gave her an innocent look as he opened the car door. "I was just remembering the eleventh verse of Proverbs 19."

"Might as well get it over with. You won't be happy until you share it with me," Daisy said, sliding in front of him into the driver's seat.

" 'The discretion of a man deferreth his anger; and it is his glory to pass over a transgression.' "

"Thankfully, I'm not a man."

Jack rolled his eyes and loped around to the passenger side.

While she drove to the club, Daisy chattered about her plans for fixing up Lou's house, as if the whole issue was a *fait accompli*.

"I'll bet the house hasn't been painted since her husband, Harry, was alive. That's the first thing—once we get a new roof and the porch repaired and a ramp built and the fence fixed, of course. And then we can start on the inside. I'd like to see it a pale yellow, maybe pick up the color in a flowered chintz on the couch." She glanced at Jack. "I love yellow. It's such a happy color."

"I wonder if Lou loves yellow," Jack murmured, looking straight ahead.

Daisy stopped talking. For a tense moment or two she was silent then gave him a sidelong smile. "Good point. It might be wise to consult with Lou before redecorating her home."

Jack began to laugh. "You're a clever girl, Daisy. I have no doubt you'll be able to convince her your choices are hers."

Daisy looked sheepish. "I do have a way of bulldozing my way ahead, don't I?"

It was Jack's turn to smile. "So far, it's worked very well for you."

"Sometimes." For a moment, she looked pensive.

He and Daisy were already seated when Daniel

entered the club dining room.

Jack could see him waiting in the entry while the headwaiter became suddenly obsessed with busywork at his lectern. It almost appeared that he was purposefully failing to notice Daniel. And his response, when Daniel finally did engage him, seemed less than gracious. "How can a headwaiter keep his job if he treats the members that way?" Jack said to Daisy.

"He doesn't treat the other members that way." Daisy placed her coffee cup back into its saucer. "Daniel was a conscientious objector during the war. That man had two sons in the army. One of them came home without a leg."

She smiled as Daniel approached. Beneath her breath she said, "Unfortunately, Daniel's had to get used to that kind of treatment. The majority of the club feels the same way toward him."

"That's why he wasn't at the party Saturday."

Daisy nodded.

When Daniel arrived at the table, he gave a wry glance over his shoulder. "I hope your service won't suffer on my account." He pulled out the chair next to Daisy.

"If it does, they'll hear from me." Daisy picked up her menu.

Daniel put a folder in the seat beside him and looked at Jack. "Did Daisy fill you in?"

"Of course I filled him in. He's my spiritual advisor." She smiled at Daniel over the top of the menu.

Daniel pulled his napkin into his lap. "You can see why I usually eat at Feingold's Deli."

"It's most bachelors' local restaurant of choice," Jack said. "Certainly mine. We could just as well have met there."

"We could, but Daisy wanted to make a point." Daniel picked up his menu.

"How's that?"

"She's my champion and wants everyone to know it." He looked around the spacious, near-empty, dining room. "It's a shame there's not a crowd." He folded his menu and put it in front of the empty place. "I know what I'm having."

Jack did likewise. "If it's eggs Benedict, I'm having the same."

"It is. The one thing that is better here than at Feingold's."

"Well, I'm having waffles with strawberries and whipped cream," Daisy said, handing her menu to Jack.

"Sounds nutritious," Jack said.

Daisy wrinkled her nose at him.

When the waiter had taken their orders, Daniel reached into the folder beside him. "Might as well get our business out of the way." He brought out a sheet on which some notes had been scratched, then cleared his throat. "This should interest you, Jack. The property is being deeded to Good Shepherd Community Church—"

"What?" Jack interrupted. "That's impossible!"

Daniel held up his hand. "Let me finish. I think you'll understand." He continued. "With the following stipulations: Lou Green is to remain in possession of her home and gardens for as long as she lives; the service station and garage are to continue to be staffed by members of the church high school group and community youth. Rick Sharky will continue as manager. The income from the garage will be used to provide for Lou Green's needs for the duration of her life."

"In other words," Jack said, "the church will act as Lou's trustee for as long as she lives." He was beginning to see that this was more a responsibility than a gift. "Why do I detect Daisy's hand in all of this?"

"Because it is." Daniel's solemn expression twitched into a smile. "These were her suggestions which I presented to the consortium, and they agreed." He glanced down at the paper. "One more thing. The attached half acre on the rear of the property has been deeded separately to the church for a youth facility. When half the amount of money necessary to build the facility is raised, the funds will be matched by the consortium."

Jack sat back in his chair, speechless.

"Well," Daisy said. "Say something. What do you think?"

"I don't know what to think. It's. . .it's amazing." He shook his head. "It's fantastic!"

While it was still sinking in, the waiter arrived with their orders and refilled their coffee cups.

Daisy burrowed into the whipped cream, stabbed a strawberry, popped it into her mouth, and chewed thoughtfully. "I wish we could do something about that unscrupulous banker, Sherm. Sweep him off the streets so he can't do the same thing to other little old ladies in his convalescent hospitals."

"Convalescent hospitals?" Daniel looked up from cutting into his slice of Canadian bacon.

"He owns a string of them," Daisy said. "Fairhaven, where Lou is, and then there's Homewood, and. . ." She thought for a moment. "What's that one near Pomona, Jack?"

"Havenhurst," he answered absently, still somewhat in a daze.

"You're not eating," she said. "You've got to eat. Keep up your strength. Make you big and strong."

Daniel was still looking at Daisy, knife poised above his Canadian bacon. "Is this guy's name Sherman Locksley, by any chance?"

"By every chance." Daisy put down her fork. "What do you know about him?"

"So the man I was bidding against was Sherman Locksley." He shook his head. "Well, what do you know." Putting down his knife and fork, the attorney sat back in his chair. A small smile twitched about his lips. He glanced to either side, then leaned forward. "This isn't for publication." His voice was low. "But Daisy might get her wish to have that unscrupulous banker out of commission sooner than she expects."

Jack and Daisy pushed their chairs closer.

"How do you think he got the money to build that string of convalescent hospitals?" Daniel said.

"How?" Daisy and Jack asked in unison.

"Off the backs of Japanese clients of mine. Sherman Locksley is under investigation for illegally seizing the property of Japanese-American citizens who were sent to concentration camps during the war."

"Another reason Daniel is persona non grata around here," Daisy said to Jack. "He does pro bono work in reparation cases." She smiled proudly at Daniel. "The man is a fanatic for embracing unpopular causes."

"So that's why Sherm Locksley called you Daisy's 'loser lawyer.'" Jack looked at the man with heightened respect. "I think I'd take that as a compliment. If there's ever anything I can do to help, Daniel, let me know."

With the tip of her tongue, Daisy daintily licked a dollop of whipped cream from the corner of her mouth, then looked from him to the lawyer. "Here I am sitting between two of the handsomest best friends a girl could have."

Jack smiled. That was nice.

Even nicer if he'd been in a class by himself.

twenty

On the way back from the country club, Daisy suggested they visit Lou.

"I think we should plan our strategy before we go in," she said, pulling her car into a parking slot at the Fairhaven Convalescent Hospital.

Jack agreed. "Lou's such an independent, proud woman. We don't want her to feel like she's accepting charity."

Daisy turned off the engine. "But how do we do that?"

For a number of minutes they sat in thoughtful silence.

"What if we make her think she's doing *us* a favor?" Daisy said slowly.

"Wouldn't that would be a bit of a stretch?"

"Not necessarily. Think about it. The girls would have an opportunity to put their new sewing skills into practice, helping to decorate Lou's house. My brother's gardener would love using her garden to give the boys horticulture classes; he's a genius with plants and wonderful with kids. In addition, they'd gain building skills constructing the ramp and replacing the porch rail and picket fence." She glanced over at Jack. "Of course we'll get a professional contractor to do the roof."

"Your friend Greg?"

Daisy nodded. "I know if I asked him, he'd do anything to help—"

"No doubt."

She was getting excited, the ideas apparently flowing faster than she could get them out. "And I'll bet we could get some of the adults in the church involved, too. What could be more Christian? Everyone working together on a cause greater than themselves. How does it sound so far?"

"Keep talking, Daisy. I think you're on a roll."

"The kids have already named it the Lou Project. We can paint the garage and service station, too, and build a planter box for flowers out in front."

Jack smiled. "A Daisy touch."

"We don't have to have flowers." She took a deep breath and started in again. "And when we're finished fixing up the house and station we start raising money for the youth facility. Keep the momentum going. We can have car washes and spaghetti dinners and craft bazaars with things the girls have made. Maybe the boys could create things out of wood, provide services, like mowing lawns and cleaning tool sheds. All toward the building fund. And. . ."

⁂

Moments later, Jack was shaking his head.

"Too much?" Daisy felt a shaft of disappointment. "You don't think it's a good idea."

"On the contrary, I think it's an *amazing* idea." His arm rested along the back of the seat. He reached out and touched her shoulder. "And I think you're an *amazing* woman."

Woman! He called me a woman.

He must not have realized what he was saying.

Or maybe she'd misheard him. Yes, that was probably it.

She didn't want to look at him—wanted the lovely illusion to last a little longer.

She became acutely aware of his hand resting on her shoulder.

Unable to help herself, she lifted her gaze.

Jack's smile was warm and appreciative. "You are an amazing woman," he repeated softly.

Well, there was no doubt this time. Her ears had not deceived her.

Jack dropped his hand and looked out the window, breaking the spell. Intentionally, it seemed to her. There had been a moment, just a moment when their gazes had locked, and she'd felt a pull of possibility.

And then he'd dropped his hand and looked out the window.

It was over, once again leaving her to wonder if it were so, or just her hopeful heart deceiving her.

"It's getting too hot to sit out here," Jack said. "Let's go inside."

He got out and came around to Daisy's side of the car. "I think you've come up with the right approach," he said, opening the car door. "It'll benefit the kids, the whole church. Maybe even more than it benefits Lou. It's a dynamic idea, Daisy."

"You probably would have thought of it, or something just as good," she said.

"I doubt it. And certainly not as full-blown and comprehensive."

They were hurrying across the parking lot. The sun had reached its zenith and heat radiated from the cement like a mirage in the desert.

Jack ushered Daisy into the shadowy foyer of the convalescent hospital. The temperature was just a few degrees lower than it was outside. "Someday they'll figure out a better way to cool these places," he said.

As they walked down the hall, he said, "I think you're the one to carry the ball, Daisy. Do you mind?"

"That's fine."

Lou looked like a wizened gray elf sitting in a lounge chair next to the bed, her legs draped with a plaid blanket that Daisy had brought when they'd moved her there. A magazine lay open on her lap.

Her face lit up at the sight of them. "P. J. and the flower. What are you doin' here? You just paid me a visit yesterday."

"First of all, I brought you a treat." Daisy went over and kissed the old lady's parchment cheek. She laid a waxed paper wrapped package on top of the magazine. *Popular Mechanics*, she noticed. "We just came back from brunch. I know how you like brownies, so I ordered a couple to take with us."

"Ain't that sweet of you." Lou opened the package and grinned. "These are as big as my front porch. Should last until your next visit. That is if I hide 'em from Rosa.

She's the night nurse. And does she have an appetite."
Lou waved her hand. "Sit down you two."

Daisy perched on the bed next to her.

"How are you feeling today, Lou?" Jack asked, pulling
up the only other chair in the room.

" 'Bout the same. It's slow going." She stuck out her
chin. "But I ain't givin' up."

Jack leaned over and covered Lou's hands with his.
"We've brought you some, what I think is, good news.
Daisy's going to tell you about it."

Jack sat as he was, squeezing Lou's hands, smiling
encouragement, as Daisy launched into the day's dra-
matic events and the plans for the future.

"That is if it's agreeable with you," Daisy said. "The
truth is, Lou, you'd be doing us a tremendous favor."

"The church needs a good project to sink its teeth
into. It brings people together," Jack said.

"Well." Lou collapsed back in her chair. "You two
sure had an adventure. I only wish I coulda been there to
see the look on that lousy banker's face when he lost the
property."

Jack laughed. "Better if you'd seen the way Daisy lit
into him."

"Good fer you, girl." Lou slapped Daisy's knee.

"Well, what do you say? Are you going to help us?"
Daisy asked.

"A course I'm gonna help you. You knew I would."

"It's settled, then." Daisy hopped down from the bed
and planted another kiss on Lou's cheek. "As soon as we
leave here, the plan goes into action."

Jack stood, then bent and lifted the old lady's weathered hands to his lips. When he tried to release her, Lou wouldn't let go.

"Ya almost make me want to be a churchgoer, P. J." With a hint of tears sparkling in her eyes, she reached for Daisy's hand as well. "You two are like my own family—after Betty and Boots, of course."

They could still hear her cackling laugh as they departed down the hall.

When they got back to the church, Daisy parked in front under an oak tree. She looked at her watch. "Can you believe it's almost three thirty? I've got to get home. My masseuse is coming in a half hour."

"I've got to go, too," Jack said, opening the car door and stepping out onto the curb. He looked down at her, his arms akimbo. "You know, Daisy, I'm counting on you to be in charge of this."

Daisy looked up at him. She was committed to the cause, that was for sure. And she knew she could do it. But she could also see her life spread out in front of her, still involved with Jack's projects five, ten years from now, when she was thirty, thirty-five. . .

Still nothing more than Jack's friend.

She'd been thinking about it since yesterday while waiting for him in the church narthex. When the reality had struck her. When she'd realized it was time to move on.

The more she thought about it, the more New York made sense.

If she stayed here, if she didn't make a clean break,

she'd be pining over Jack McCutcheon until they were both in their graves.

And they would still just be friends.

"Of course, Jack." She sighed. "I'll be happy to organize the Lou Project. Get it started. Though I doubt I'll be here for the completion of the youth facility. I've decided it's time I expand my horizons. I expect I'll be moving to New York in the fall."

twenty-one

"Moving to New York?" Jack got back in the car. "You've got to be kidding."

"No, I'm not."

He looked at her dumbly. "You're kidding. Why would you want to do that?"

"Don't look so shocked."

He was not just shocked, he was alarmed. Losing Daisy was like losing an arm or a leg, she was so much a part of his life—that is—the life of the church.

"I can't believe it. Why would you suddenly do such a crazy thing?"

"Why is it so crazy? You're the one who said I should do something constructive with my life. Broaden my horizons."

"I didn't mean move to New York. Besides, I said broaden your *interests*, not your horizons."

"A semantic difference."

"Oh, you've got to be kidding." He laughed, but it sounded hollow—or was it hopeful? "A joke, right?"

Daisy sighed. "I'm not joking. It's not a sudden decision. I've been considering it for some time. Sunday, when I was waiting for you I realized what a rut I'm in. You were right, I need to start thinking of my future. Do something constructive with my life."

"And you have." Jack leaned forward. "What could be

more constructive than what you've done right here at Good Shepherd Community Church? You've made a real impact."

"I appreciate your saying that."

"You know it's true. And there's so much more that needs doing."

"I'm not going for at least two months. Don't worry, I won't leave you in the lurch."

"I'm not implying that's the only rationale for you to stay."

"I know that."

"I could write a book on all the reasons."

She looked away. "It's time. I'm spinning my wheels here, Jack. I've got to move on with my life. And I can't do it here. I need to make new friends, meet new people."

"What's wrong with the old ones?"

"Nothing." She hesitated. "But, I'll be twenty-five my next birthday—"

"If it's a party you want—"

"Don't be sarcastic, Jack. I'm getting older—"

"Real old."

"Stop interrupting." Daisy glared at him. "All my friends are married. I'd like to meet someone and fall in love, too. Get married. Have children."

"You don't have to go to New York to find a husband. There are plenty of young men right here. Why, I'd bet there are a dozen in your country club just waiting for some encouragement. Greg, for one."

Daisy stared at him. She pushed the key into the ignition. "Get out, Jack. I've got to go."

"You're angry."

"No. Just tired." She put the car in gear. "I'll talk to you later." When he shut the door, she gunned the motor and sped off—without looking back.

She was angry, all right. He could read her like a book. He knew everything about her.

But he wondered what he'd said to upset her so.

Bemused, he stood on the curb, watching until the little yellow sports car turned the corner and was out of sight.

As he walked back to his office he pondered what it would be like without Daisy.

Not a pleasant thought.

Sure, she was too spontaneous and not always practical, but she wasn't crazy.

The idea of Daisy ending up in New York was not only crazy, it was laughable. She was a California girl, born and bred, in and out.

If she did go, she wouldn't last long. She'd hightail it back to California at the first chill. Besides, she was too attached to her manicurist and hairdresser, her masseuse, her decorator. . . Not to mention all the kids and Court and Rebecca and her set at the country club.

And all the other people who cared about her.

No, she wouldn't last a month in New York.

Unless she fell in love. Then she'd be gone forever.

Forever. That was a long time.

It was too depressing to think about.

Jack barely acknowledged Mrs. Beemer as he stomped into his office.

The rest of the afternoon, all he could think about was Daisy leaving.

twenty-two

The moment the elevator door to her penthouse opened, Tiffany pounced.

Daisy leaned down and cuddled her furry canine, allowing wet kisses to be slathered over her cheeks. "What one will do for love," she murmured, burying her face in the dog's ruff.

Martha, her housekeeper, walked into the foyer, pulling on her gloves. "I already took Tiffany out, so you won't have to bother until bedtime."

"Thanks, Martha."

The plump, red-haired woman adjusted her hat in front of the Louis XIV gilt mirror over the antique credenza. "Helga called. Her car broke down so she won't be able to give you a massage today. She'll get in touch later in the week to set up another appointment." Martha pushed the elevator's down button. "See you tomorrow."

The elevator door barely slid closed when the telephone rang. Daisy picked it up in the kitchen.

"Hi, Daisy, it's Jack."

Jack.

Hadn't he done enough damage for one day? She was still smarting from his attempts at marriage brokering. It would have been funny if it hadn't hurt so much.

However, it had strengthened her resolve to leave.

"I'm sorry," he said. "I'm not exactly sure what for, but I don't want you to be unhappy."

How could he understand other people so well, and be so clueless when it came to understanding her?

Maybe, subconsciously, it was intentional. Maybe he didn't see what he didn't want to see.

"You don't need to apologize."

She tried to concentrate on scratching behind Tiffany's ears.

"I've been thinking some more about your going to New York," he said. "From a selfish standpoint, of course, I'd rather you didn't. It'll take at least three people to replace you. Even then, it won't be the same. But it's your life, and you have to do what you think is best. You know I'll support whatever decision you make."

I've already made it, Jack. "Thanks, I appreciate that."

"I'm also calling to make a date to pay on our wager."

Daisy sighed. "The bet was just for fun. You don't need to do anything." Somehow, it didn't matter anymore.

"No, I want to. How about Wednesday after class?"

Of course it wouldn't be on a Friday or Saturday. That might be construed as a date.

"Fine. Hope it's not formal, since I won't have time to go home and shower."

Jack laughed.

He sounded relieved at her lame attempt at humor. Things were getting back to normal.

"Douse on that lilac scent you wear, and I'll never know the difference."

So he had noticed her lilac perfume. That was a step in the right direction.

Too late.

❧

Daisy dressed carefully Wednesday afternoon, wondering why it still mattered so much. She wore the pink-and-white polka-dot sleeveless dress with the wide belt and the circular skirt and her matching sandals. Jack had complimented her on the outfit the day they'd picnicked in the park.

She had been to the church manse many times before, but always with groups of people or for a casual evening with mutual friends. Court and Rebecca were usually at those events.

Rebecca, her dearest friend. Her nemesis.

But this was the first time she'd been there alone.

Even though it would be a couple of months before she left, in a way this evening was kind of a good-bye. The period at the end of a sentence.

She tied a pink ribbon in her hair and dabbed the lilac perfume behind each ear, at her throat and wrists.

Maybe when she was gone and he got a whiff of lilac, he'd remember her. . .and be a little sorry.

❧

Daisy's heart thumped faster as she ascended the front porch steps of the two-story wood-frame manse.

Jack must have heard her because the door opened before she had a chance to ring the bell.

He stood in the entry, tall and so handsome it took her breath away. He wore a white golf shirt that set off his tan and emphasized, in a way the dark clerical shirt never had, the breadth of his shoulders, the definition of his strong, muscled arms.

His sun-bleached hair was still damp from the shower.

In his dark eyes she detected a glimmer of unease before his smile broke.

Was it possible he shared her apprehension?

"You look lovely, Daisy," he said, pushing open the screen door and drawing her into the living room. "I'm glad you're here."

"I'm glad to be here."

Aren't we being formal. So well-behaved.

She glanced around the room, seeing it for the first time unadorned with people: the oak-stained walls, the stone fireplace, the eclectic mishmash of hand-me-down furniture; every piece slipcovered or upholstered in a faded, threadbare fabric.

Even the drapes were shabby!

Oh, how she would like to sink her teeth into this decorator's challenge. She envied the wife who eventually would.

Jack was watching her. "Mrs. Beemer found a bargain."

She couldn't help smiling. "And here I was giving you all the credit."

Soft music played in the background, a Beethoven sonata. On the coffee table in front of the couch a nosegay of pink carnations sprouted from a cut glass vase. He'd even lighted votive candles. There was a tray with cheese and crackers, a bowl of mixed nuts, and two iced glasses of lemonade.

So far he'd thought of everything.

"I'm overwhelmed," she said to his diffident smile.

If she hadn't known better, she might have thought he was trying to impress her.

He sat down beside her on the couch. Close enough that if she moved her knee a fraction they would touch.

She imagined she could feel his heat.

He handed her a glass of lemonade and lifted the other for himself. "How was your class?"

Daisy took a sip of the tart beverage. "You would have laughed. The girls teased me about being all dressed up. Gave me the third degree."

"Did you tell them where you were going?"

"Are you kidding?"

"Ashamed to be seen with me?"

"Of course not. I just didn't think you would want it to be a matter of discussion at the next church board meeting."

"Such chances we take." He grinned.

Their ease was gradually returning.

He touched his glass to hers. "Here's to your happiness, Daisy. Wherever you find it."

"To your happiness, too." *Whoever she may be.*

What was that prayer? "God grant me the serenity to accept the things I cannot change. . . ." *Please, God.*

Daisy put down her glass and spread a cracker with the soft cheese. Handing it to Jack, she made another for herself.

She took a bite. "Mmm, that's delicious. Gorgonzola. My favorite."

"It has been ever since you were three." He laughed. "Like pink."

"I guess I have more sophisticated taste in food than in colors."

"They both look good on you," he said, wiping a crumb from the corner of her mouth with his thumb.

His touch made her tremble. She didn't want it to show. She sat back and looked at him over the rim of her glass. "There are some wonderful scents wafting from the direction of the kitchen. What has the chef prepared for dinner?"

"It's a surprise."

"Whatever it is, you certainly are casual about it. I would have thought you'd be slaving away in the kitchen."

"Almost everything's ready. It'll just take a minute to put it on the table."

"You sound so domestic, Jack."

"I'm not totally a lost cause."

Daisy studied her lemonade. She couldn't bring herself to respond.

Before the moment became awkward, Jack stood up. "Are you getting hungry?"

"Let me help." She started to rise, but he pushed her gently back onto the couch.

"This is my party," he said, looking quite serious. "You are to act like a guest."

"Honestly, I really would like to help."

"Humor me!" His tone brooked no argument.

"Don't I always?" She made a face at his retreating

back and picked up a magazine.

It engaged her only for a minute or two before she returned it to the coffee table, stood up, and walked over to the bookcase flanking the fireplace. She scanned the varied collection that reflected Jack's curious mind, his intellect. His spirituality.

Her fingers drifted over the spines of books on history, philosophy, religion, the complete works of Shakespeare and Dickens, contemporary novels, and tomes on critical thinking.

She touched the books around which he had wrapped his big hands, his mind, and his generous heart.

Tears threatened, but she blinked them back.

Jack was beside her.

"*The Screwtape Letters* by C. S. Lewis." He reached over her shoulder and pulled it from the shelf. "It's a wonderful book. If you haven't read it, I'll lend it to you."

"Thanks, I haven't. It certainly had good reviews."

"You won't be disappointed."

He was so close. She could smell the faint aroma of his lemony-scented aftershave.

So close, if she'd leaned back, she would have been resting against his chest. What a natural thing to do.

If she had, she would have landed on the floor. Jack had already stepped back. He made a slight bow from the waist. "Dinner is served, madam."

The moment was lost.

He opened the door to the dining room. "Ta da!"

Daisy could hardly believe her eyes.

A linen cloth covered the table. Lighted candles and a

mixed bouquet of roses—"Swiped from Lou's garden," Jack confessed—were in the center, the place settings, perfect.

"It's beautiful, Jack. One would almost think you had taken my Bible study class." She slipped into the chair he had pulled out for her.

The first course was already at each place: jellied consommé in half a honeydew melon, garnished with a slice of lime.

"The perfect starter for a summer dinner," she said as Jack cleared the plates for the salad course. "I can't believe it. You even know how to serve: serve to the right, clear from the left."

"I was a server in college in a sorority."

A minute later he returned with two salads in one hand and a covered basket of biscuits in the other.

Daisy giggled. "Now I see shades of your past training."

"French green salad," he announced, setting a plate in front of her.

After her first bite of the main course—an impressive Chicken Parisienne on rice, accompanied by minted peas—Daisy said, "I had no idea you had such culinary skills."

"Wait until you see the dessert."

"Don't tell me it's flaming."

"I'm not that ambitious. Do you want coffee?" he asked, clearing their dishes.

"That would be lovely. You're sure I can't help?"

"Absolutely not! All I have to do is turn on the heat under the coffee."

Daisy didn't think she could eat another bite, until she saw it. "Floating Island! Jack, you're amazing. And with strawberries."

"You must have been working on this dinner for days," she said, having polished off every bite of the delicious dessert. She wiped the corner of her mouth and lifted her cup of the steaming brew. "You're coffee is excellent, too. Not too weak and not too strong but. . ."

"Just right," they said in unison and laughed.

"One would think you were auditioning for host of the year."

She wondered why he'd wasted it on her.

Jack had changed the record on the phonograph to a Horowitz recording of Chopin's nocturnes.

For several minutes they listened in silence as they sipped their coffee.

He put down his cup and leaned back in his chair. His hand that rested on the table moved over to cover hers. "You're very good company, Daisy. I'm going to miss you if you go to New York."

She held her breath.

"I wish there were something I could say to make you change your mind."

Daisy had the chiming doorbell to thank for keeping her from blurting out the truth.

twenty-three

"You answer the door. I'll clear the dishes," Daisy said, picking up her dessert plate.

"No, Daisy," Jack said adamantly. He took it from her and set it back on the table.

The doorbell chimed again.

Jack took her hand and drew her back into the living room, then opened the front door.

"Mrs. Parrott. Virgie. What a surprise."

Daisy's heart sank. If she thought this evening would be fodder for the girls in Bible study class it was nothing compared to the tidal wave that would wash through the church when Mavis Parrott saw her. As she was about to do.

"Won't you come in?" Jack said, stepping aside and pushing open the screen door.

The two women stood in the light of the porch lamp, one bosomy and robust, the other her frail replica.

"Chocolate chip cookies for you, Pastor." Mrs. Parrott held up an overflowing plate, urging her daughter to move forward. It was obvious that Mrs. Parrott was more interested in passing off Virgie than the treats.

Poor Virgie stood in embarrassed silence, her eyes cast down at her sensible oxfords.

"The Altar Guild ladies begged Virgie to make her famous cookies for their meeting. I said, 'Virgie, why don't you make some extras for the pastor. A poor bachelor, having to cook for himself and all. . .'"

"That was thoughtful of you, Virgie." Jack smiled at the girl.

Well, not exactly a girl. She looked to be at least thirty-two or -three. Several years older than Daisy.

Mavis Parrott suddenly noticed Daisy. Her toothy smile slumped into a disapproving line. "Oh, I see you have a guest."

"Hello, Mrs. Parrott. Virgie." Daisy stepped forward to greet them.

Mrs. Parrott took a step back, pulling her daughter behind her as if shielding her from the brazen hussy in the pink dress and polished nails.

She peered around Daisy into the dining room. "Oh. How embarrassing. I can see that we interrupted an intimate little dinner."

Intimate little dinner. Don't I wish.

Jack glanced at Daisy.

Oh no. He knew as well as she did where this was heading. But what could he do? The church's resident busybody would sink her teeth into this little encounter like a chocolate lover into a bonbon.

"Not really a party, Mrs. Parrott. Paying back a wager of sorts. Daisy and I had—"

"You don't have to explain to me, Pastor," Mrs. Parrott said, backing out the door.

"You're sure you and Virgie won't stay for coffee?"

"Oh, no. Virgie and I would never think of imposing. Come along, dear."

Jack flashed the hapless younger woman a compassionate smile as her mother, still clutching the plate of chocolate chip cookies, dragged her across the porch and down the front steps.

"Hope to see you Sunday in church," Jack called, closing the door.

He turned to Daisy. "Well, so much for a romantic evening."

"Oh," Daisy said lightly. "Is that what you had in mind?"

"Just kidding." He grinned. "Don't worry, Daisy dear, your virtue is safe with me."

"There was never a doubt."

"Only in Mavis Parrott's mind," Jack said, frowning. "It'll be interesting to see what she makes of this."

If only it were true. "Won't it. I'd better go," Daisy said.

Jack walked her out to her little yellow sports car waiting by the curb.

She leaned against the car. "Your dinner was wonderful, Jack, and I had a great time."

"I did, too, Daisy."

"I really would like your recipe for that chicken. It was delicious."

Jack laughed. "I never thought I'd be asked for a recipe."

"Now that you've had a successful dry run with me, you can put it in your arsenal for attracting the ladies."

"I don't think so. Anyway"—he gave her arm an

affectionate squeeze—"I really had a great evening."

"So did I."

It was a clear night. Twinkling stars. Full moon. The gardenia bushes near the house filled the air with their heavy scent. Every now and then a car whooshed by, drowning out the crickets' serenade.

"Well, I'd better go."

"I suppose," Jack said. He leaned forward to give her his usual brotherly kiss on the cheek.

Daisy, recklessly, turned her head.

Their lips met.

And lingered. Gentle. Tender.

She found her arms around his neck. She clung to him, smelling the scent of him, feeling his warmth.

Jack suddenly pulled away. "Daisy, I am so sorry. I apologize. I don't know what happened."

"Oh, honestly, Jack." She jumped into her car and slammed the door. "You didn't do anything. I made it happen. I've been waiting for that kiss for twenty-five years, and I'm only twenty-four. If you have anything to apologize for it's that, after all my waiting, it didn't last long enough."

She twisted the key in the ignition, threw the car into gear, and laid rubber.

The only thing she left behind was her pride.

twenty-four

That night, thoughts of Daisy kept Jack awake.

What troubled him most was his response to her kiss. The way he'd warmed to the soft touch of her lips, their sweet taste as they moved with such gentle insistence against his own.

How willingly he had allowed himself to be drawn into her embrace.

He had pondered her outburst. It didn't take much imagination to see that for a long time there had been signs of her feelings for him. Signs that he had chosen to interpret as sisterly affection. Signs that he had dismissed with the childhood nickname, Ditsi.

Ditsi.

How could anyone called Ditsi be taken seriously?

That was the point.

He hadn't wanted to take her seriously.

Now he had no choice.

These were the thoughts tangling in his brain when Mrs. Beemer confronted him in his office the following morning. The expression on her face warned him.

"So. What did you hear?" he asked.

Mrs. Beemer sang, "Your secret love's no secret anymore."

"Very funny."

"You know how it is. A piece of juicy gossip spreads through our little congregation faster than the Israelites fled Egypt. Bulletin: Unmarried minister entertains single young woman in his home. At night. Unchaperoned. What's more—are you ready?"

Jack sagged down on the edge of her desk. He figured he knew what was coming next.

"What's more, said minister and single woman kissed. . . *passionately*"—Mrs. Beemer paused for effect—"in front of the whole neighborhood and all passing cars."

Jack groaned. "A slight exaggeration, to say the least."

"Who wants to believe that?" Mrs. Beemer leaned back in her chair. "This is very damaging, Pastor Jack. Not just for you, but for her."

"That woman's gone too far this time." Jack's anger propelled him to his feet.

He was a man. He could take it. But it was so unfair to dear little Ditsi.

His fists clenched. His whole body tensed.

"As I see it," Mrs. Beemer said, "there's only one way to handle this."

"What?"

"You've got to save the lady's reputation."

"And how do you propose I should do that?"

"Pastor, Pastor, Pastor. Have you no imagination? Or is there a lack of red blood cells running through your veins?"

"Very amusing, Mrs. Beemer."

Jack stalked into his office where he remained secluded the rest of the morning and into the afternoon, ostensibly to work on next Sunday's sermon.

About three o'clock there was a knock on his office door.

"More good news, Pastor."

"Come in, Mrs. Beemer."

This time she wasn't smiling. "It seems the telephone tree has been at work. The church board is calling an open meeting of the congregation tomorrow night for the purpose of looking into the minister's indiscretions."

Mrs. Beemer crossed her arms, her expression fierce. "Plain and simple, Pastor Jack, it's an inquisition. That Parrott woman is behind it."

Jack rocked back. He put his elbows on the chair's arms and steepled his fingers.

"How can you remain so calm?" Mrs. Beemer squeaked. "Your job, your reputation—Daisy's reputation is at stake."

"I'm well aware of that," he said quietly. "I've been struggling with it all day. I was reading the Bible and came across the fifth chapter of Matthew, verse forty-four. You remember the one. 'But I say unto you, Love your enemies, bless them that curse you, do good to them that hate you, and pray for them which despite-fully use you, and persecute you.' I'm a minister, Mrs. Beemer. It's not easy, but if I can't pull that off, then I'm in the wrong profession."

"You're a better man than I am," Mrs. Beemer sniffed.

"Then there's good old John chapter eight, verse thirty-two: 'And ye shall know the truth, and the truth shall make you free.'"

Jack stood up and walked around his desk. He put his arm around the gray-haired church secretary. "I've got God on my side, and I've got you. A winning combination.

"Let them bring on my Goliath."

twenty-five

Jack had tried to reach Daisy numerous times by phone, without success. He'd even gone to her apartment. No answer there, either. Though he thought he saw Tiffany's nose peeking over the wall of the balcony. Which made him suspect Daisy might be home.

Finally, he called Court and Rebecca. No luck. Although they did say they would be at the meeting Friday night to support him.

The meeting was to start at 8:00, but by 7:30, the fellowship hall was crowded. In fact, there was standing room only. Baby-sitting had been provided so that young parents could attend. The teenagers clustered in the hall outside, showing their support for Pastor Jack and Daisy, even though they were not allowed inside during the meeting.

Folding chairs had been set up with a narrow aisle down the middle. There was a long table in front for the church board. At the side was a chair designated for him.

Someone had placed a placard on it so no one else would sit there.

The appointed hour arrived. The board took their places. Jack took his.

A few muffled coughs and nervous whispers echoed as the crowd grew quiet.

From the front row, Court gave Jack the high sign.

Jack smiled. They'd been doing that since grade school.

The meeting was brought to order, and the moderator called on Jack to give a brief invocation—which seemed to Jack a bit hypocritical on the board's part, under the circumstances.

There was a shuffling of feet as everyone rose and bowed their heads.

Jack began, "Dear Lord, may we maintain a calm composure that speaks of our trust in the outworking of Your order and harmony. As it is said in Galatians five, twenty-five: 'If we live in the Spirit, let us also walk in the Spirit.' Amen."

"Amen." Again the shuffling feet and quiet whispers as the congregation settled back into their seats.

Jack spoke first. In a tone of calm conviction, he explained how he, Court, and Daisy had been friends since childhood. How he had been treated as a member of the Fielding family and thought of Daisy as his little sister. "Younger sister. Well, *little*, too."

Those who were acquainted with the diminutive Daisy smiled.

He told of their wager and how he had agreed to prepare Daisy a homemade dinner if she increased the size of the girls' Bible study class. "And, as everyone here knows," he said, "her efforts far exceeded our expectations."

A murmur of agreement passed through the audience.

"The reason for the dinner, which, I might say has

been greatly misinterpreted, was to honor our agreement." With that, Jack sat down.

There was a smattering of supporting applause.

The moderator hit his gavel for silence.

Then Mavis Parrot had her turn. She stood up, holding a paper on which she had made her notes for rebuttal.

"Let us first address the matter of the Bible study class, which I have thoroughly investigated. I personally do not feel that makeup, posture, and hairdos constitute a study of the Good Book." She added a few more points in her derisive assessment and moved to the next issue.

"The matter of the intimate, *unchaparoned* dinner. I ask you. What kind of a woman would go alone at night to a bachelor's house?" She raised her hand and shook her finger. "I ask you. What kind of woman would stand in a public thoroughfare and kiss a man, *passionately*." Her bosom heaved as she took a deep breath. "And finally, what kind of minister would allow it? Ask yourselves this: Do we want a man of such poor judgment leading our flock?" Mrs. Parrott folded her notes and flounced back to her chair.

Jack leaped to his feet. He was not about to allow Daisy's name to be dragged through the mud. Forget the invocation's call for calm and composure.

"Think what you will of me, but Daisy Fielding is one of the finest human beings I have ever known. I cannot imagine this church without her. What she has done for the youth of this community is phenomenal." He gave a *complete* report and analysis of the Bible study

class, and he told about Lou and how Daisy was orga-
nizing the young people to help her and about the plan
for a youth facility.

"None of this would have happened if it weren't for
Daisy Fielding.

"Why, Daisy is a woman of the highest values and
virtues." He listed them, one by one. "Her every deed is
in the interest of others, her every action above reproach."

Only when Mrs. Beemer, who was sitting in the middle of the audience, stood up, did he realize that he was
on a roll that was not about to run down.

"Pastor Jack, may I have a word?"

"By all means, Mrs. Beemer."

Mrs. Beemer made her way across the row and down
the center aisle.

With her steely gray hair and sturdy frame, she exem-
plified a church "pillar," if there ever was one. And she
was respected as such. When Mrs. Beemer spoke, she
inspired trust.

She stood before the congregation, her feet slightly
apart, her hands folded over her stomach, and scanned
the assemblage with her no-nonsense gaze.

"I'm going to apologize to Pastor Jack for breaking a
confidence." She glanced at him and continued. "Pastor
Jack didn't want Daisy to know that I had helped him
cook the dinner. I was the chaperone at the pastor's
intimate"—she glared at Mrs. Parrott—"dinner party.
Unbeknownst to Daisy, I was in the kitchen before she
arrived and after she left, I must add. And as for Daisy's
virtue, she was having dinner with a lifelong family

friend, not some bachelor with whom she had a casual acquaintance. I couldn't agree more with the fine things Pastor Jack said about her."

"That settles it." Rebecca jumped to her feet. "I think we all agree that there could not be a more trustworthy, reliable chaperone than Mrs. Beemer."

"Hear, hear," Court shouted, beginning to clap.

Others joined in the applause, until the whole room was stomping and clapping and shouting, "Pastor Jack, Pastor Jack. . ."

The moderator pounded his gavel, but nobody paid any attention.

From outside the fellowship hall came a faint harmony. Someone at the back of the auditorium thrust open the door and the teenage choir, which consisted of members of the girls' Bible study class and of the boys' Bible study and basketball league, plus a few more, making about forty members in all, crowded through the double doors and marched down the middle aisle and to the front of the room singing "Glory, Glory, Halleluiah." In four-part harmony.

Mavis Parrott did not stay for the performance.

twenty-six

It hit Jack like the proverbial ton of bricks.

He was in love with Daisy Fielding.

Standing in the midst of the mingling, enthusiastic crowd, the chattering and singing, he murmured silently to himself, "I'm in love with Daisy Fielding."

Somehow, just putting it into words made it a reality.

I'm in love with Daisy Fielding.

It was all he could do to keep from leaping to his feet and shouting his sudden and wondrous news: *I'm in love with Daisy Fielding!*

Discretion kept him silent—and the memory that she had not answered or returned his phone calls. When he'd gone to her apartment, she had not responded, even though he strongly suspected she was there.

Before all this trouble, he would have felt quite confident of her response. Perhaps arrogantly so, he thought with a stab of shame.

Now?

❧

Late that evening, Jack stood at Daisy's elevator buzzer as uncertain of the response he would receive as he'd been earlier.

One thing for which he was grateful, she had not been present to hear Mavis Parrott.

Much as he prayed, charitable as he tried to be, it was difficult for Jack to forgive the injustice of the accusations that had spewed from the woman's slanderous tongue.

On the other hand, her abuse of Daisy had certainly slapped him to his senses.

He couldn't wait another minute. He had to tell Daisy how he felt.

Now!

This time her voice came through the intercom. "Yes?"

"Daisy, it's Jack."

There was a pause, long enough for him to notice, before she said, "I thought it might be you. Come on up." It seemed to him her voice lacked its usual lilt of enthusiasm.

Who could blame her?

But as the elevator ascended, so did his spirits. Surely when he took her in his arms and told her how much she meant to him, that she was the most beautiful, sensitive, generous girl in the world, that he couldn't live without her—

The elevator door slid open.

Tiffany greeted him, her paws on his chest, laving his face with her wet tongue.

"Off, girl." He pushed her away. "It's not your kisses I came for."

In the dimly lit living room, Jack's gaze found Daisy, curled up at the far end of the couch, her legs tucked under her.

"Come in and sit down," she said. "I'm glad you're here."

He breathed a sigh of relief.

"Over there." She gestured toward the chair opposite her on the other side of the fireplace. "We need to talk."

"That's why I came."

His stomach was churning with. . .certainly not nervousness.

"No, I mean, *I* need to talk," Daisy said.

"Have I ever tried to stop you?" He balanced on the edge of the seat of the wingback chair. "But first, let me—"

Daisy interrupted. "I heard everything tonight."

"Everything?" *Oh, no.* His heart sank. "Where were you? I didn't see you."

"Eavesdropping behind the choir room door."

"Then you heard Mavis Parrott?"

She nodded.

"I'm sorry. You shouldn't have had to hear that."

"It was my choice. I can't believe that woman."

"Nobody can. As you saw."

"Thank you for saying those nice things about me. Even if they were a huge exaggeration that no one in their right mind would ever believe."

"Oh, my dear girl." He started to rise, but Daisy lifted a warning hand, and he sank back into the chair. "I believe every word of what I said. Mrs. Beemer does, too."

Daisy gave him a pinched smile. "No wonder you wouldn't let me go into the kitchen."

"Are you mad at me?"

"I'm not sure."

Jack leaned forward. "Daisy, please—"

"Let me just get this out, Jack, I need to say it."

He didn't know how much longer he could hold himself back. But she seemed so insistent.

"I've changed a lot, since that lunch at Feingold's."

"I don't want you to change," he murmured.

"On the inside." She put her hand over her heart. "I have to admit, my motives were far from pure when we made our wager. I wanted to show you that I wasn't just a frivolous wing nut. Even though in my heart I thought maybe you were right."

"I never said that."

"Let me finish." She gave him a stern look. "As I became more and more involved with the girls and then with what happened to Lou, I learned a lot about myself. I learned what I was capable of. I got so involved, that I forgot it had all started because I wanted to impress you."

She leaned forward. "I learned that the Lord can use even a silly girl like me to do His work."

"A silly girl like you? Oh, Daisy, you are the most beautiful and dear and. . .and humble. . ." He wanted to rush over and take her in his arms and kiss away the frown on her sweet face.

Daisy held up her hands, warding him off again. "What is that passage from the Bible about losing your life and finding it? You know. In Matthew."

" 'He that findeth his life shall lose it: and he that loseth his life for my sake shall find it.' "

"That's it. That's exactly how I feel." The frown relaxed. Her face glowed. "I feel so useful. Happy. It doesn't matter what other people say about me or whether you. . . ." She paused. "I truly have found my life."

She took a breath and fell back into the sofa's deep cushion. "There, I've said it. Thank you for listening, Jack. You're the one person I knew would understand."

Daisy had just shared with him the most life affirming realization a person can experience. There was no way he was about to interrupt this precious moment.

It was up to her to break the spell.

Still, it was all Jack could do to sit quietly and wait.

After some moments of silence, she looked up at him and smiled. "I did think that Floating Island was a bit ambitious for a beginner."

With one stride, Jack was beside her. He sat down on the couch and took her hands in his. All the words he'd rehearsed, all the eloquent phrases, forgotten.

As he looked into her trusting blue eyes, all he could think of to say was, "Daisy, I love you."

twenty-seven

"I know you love me," Daisy said. "You have since I was eight years old." She had no illusions of the kind of love he meant. "Just because of that mean Mrs. Parrott, you think you need to say it. But you don't."

"No, I mean *really* love you," Jack said. "And it has nothing to do with Mavis Parrott. All the way over here I was rehearsing how I was going to tell you. And now the moment's here, and I can't remember any of it. But that's what it boils down to, plain and simple." He cupped her face in his hands. "I love you, Daisy Fielding. And I want you to be my wife."

The words she had been waiting for all her life, and now she couldn't believe what she heard.

She looked up into Jack's brown eyes, so filled with hesitancy and hope. "You really mean it? You love me? Grown-up woman me?"

"Would you be more convinced if I got down on one knee?"

"That won't be necessary," she said demurely. But her heart was soaring. Her whole body alive with the thrill of it. In that moment she felt beautiful, empowered, free, as if this whole wondrous universe was created just for her. And for him.

Jack drew her into his arms with such gentle tenderness

as if she were a fragile blossom whose petals could be damaged with too strong a touch.

He had a lot to learn.

Daisy threw her arms around him and with an ardor born of waiting, she held him tight. "Oh, Jack, I love you, too, with all my heart. Ever since I can remember."

She tilted her head back and met his lips with hers, long and sweet and lingering until their breath was gone.

❧

From that day on, Daisy was in a frenzy of happy activity. Not only was she planning her wedding, she continued her girls' Bible study class, coordinated the Lou Project, and got bids from architects for the youth center.

"I don't know how you do it," Jack said. "With all that's going on, I can hardly get a sermon written."

"That's because I keep barging in here and pestering you." She pulled the chair in front of the desk closer, sat down, and placed her elbows on the desk and her chin on her locked fingers.

"That's not helping, Daisy, I can't get anything done with you staring at me."

"I just have a couple of things to talk over with you, and I'll be out of here."

Jack put down his pen and rocked back in his chair. "I'm at your disposal."

"First, about the guest list. There's no way, Jack, that we can leave anybody in the church out."

Jack smiled. "Even Mavis Parrott?"

"Well, we can't ask Virgie and not her mother. So if

it's all right with you, I think we should put a blanket invitation in the church bulletin. That way we won't miss anybody."

"You're the bride. It's your decision. I'm just coming along for the ride."

"That's settled then. Do you want to speak to Mrs. Beemer, or shall I?"

"You go ahead."

"Those folks who aren't church members will receive personal invitations: friends in the club, my bridge group, manicurist, hairdresser, et cetera. You'll have to give me your list as well."

"I think you've covered just about everybody. That's sure going to be a whopping reception."

"Rebecca and Court offered to give it. The estate can accommodate thousands."

"I hope that's not how many you intend to invite."

Daisy giggled. "Scared you, didn't I?"

"It was beginning to sound more like a political rally than a wedding."

Daisy consulted her mental list.

"Have you asked all your groomsmen, yet?"

Jack nodded. "I know Court's giving you away, but I still want him as my best man."

"No problem; it's our wedding. We can do anything we want. I know you were thinking of asking Daniel Essex."

"That's taken care of."

"Oh no."

"What's the matter?"

"My roommate from college moved back to take care of her mother. I asked her to be one of my attendants."

"So what's the problem?"

"Daniel and Claire used to be engaged."

"That's the woman he's carrying a torch for."

"It was pretty sad. Her brother and Daniel were best friends. He was killed in the Pacific."

"And Daniel was a conscientious objector."

"You've got it."

Jack sighed. "Well, we can't un-invite either of them. I guess it'll just have to play itself out."

That was the only cloudy spot on Daisy's otherwise sunny horizon.

She leaned forward. "Oh, one more thing. I think we should make it clear, *absolutely no gifts*. If anyone feels so inclined, they can make a donation to the building fund of the youth center. Agreed?"

"Agreed."

"We can buy our own presents. You know how I love to shop."

Ignoring his groan, she bounced up, threw him a kiss, and pranced out the door.

twenty-eight

Daisy could not have planned a more beautiful afternoon for her four o'clock wedding in early October. The California weather was balmy, the sky without a cloud.

It was as if the whole world stood at attention in celebration.

Just as she'd dreamed it, the sanctuary of the Good Shepherd Community Church had become a glorious array of flowers and ferns plucked from the gardens of the Fielding estate. They flanked the altar, dripped from the choir loft, and swagged down the middle aisle, caught by pink satin bows.

Fortunately, Daisy's friend the fire marshal was also a guest, for rows of folding chairs had been set up down the side aisles to anticipate the overflow of guests who were escorted to their seats by the dozen groomsmen and ushers.

In front of the first two rows of seats space had been saved for Lou and several other patients in wheelchairs Daisy had befriended at the convalescent hospital. Behind them sat Rick and the entire Lou's Lube and Service Station teenage staff.

The guests chatted quietly, while in the background, Mrs. Beemer, at the organ, played Pachelbel's "Canon in D" and other baroque favorites.

Through the crack between the double doors at the back of the sanctuary, Daisy watched as the youth choir, in their new white robes, entered from the side and took their seats in the choir loft, and the two rows of additional chairs that had been placed in front of it.

Everything was going just as she'd planned.

The choir rose to sing Handel's "Hallelujah Chorus," setting the tone, not only for a sanctified union, but a joyous celebration.

When Mrs. Beemer began the classic "Jesu, Joy of Man's Desiring," it was the signal for Jack and Dr. Madison, minister of Pasadena First Community, who would officiate, to enter the sanctuary.

Daisy stepped aside as the twelve ushers and groomsmen moved through the double doors, in their tuxedos and polished shoes, and marched by twos down the center aisle.

Right on schedule.

In stately beat, the eleven lovely bridesmaids followed. They wore matching pink tulle dresses with cap sleeves and satin ribbons at their waists and pearl earrings with matching pearl pendants, and carried nosegays of pink baby roses.

Daisy gave Rebecca and Court's six-year-old son, Davy, a thumbs-up as he stepped into the sanctuary. He looked adorable in his little black tuxedo, marching confidently toward his "uncle" Jack, bearing the two wedding rings on a white satin pillow.

Her heart fluttered as she watched Mrs. Beemer's granddaughter, little Mimi James, a precocious toddler with golden curls, in a pink dress that matched the bridesmaids' gowns, follow Davy, plucking rose petals from her tiny basket and tossing them out to float down onto the white satin runner.

Someday she and Jack would have their own precious children.

Rebecca, Daisy's matron of honor, leaned over and gave her a hug. "It'll be your turn next, sweetie." She smiled at her husband and floated down the aisle as she had two years before, a young widow, little Davy at her side.

The wedding coordinator, little Mimi James' mother, closed the double doors.

Daisy's stomach began to churn.

After years of waiting and weeks of excitement, the anticipated moment had arrived.

Her life would change forever. Forever. So final.

With the fanfare to the *Lohengrin* "Wedding March," she could hear the bustle of the congregation rising.

Was she really ready to do this?

Covering her hand that was tucked through his arm, Court murmured, "Break a leg, little sister. The curtain is about to go up."

"Don't be sacrilegious, Court," she whispered back, but grateful to him for easing the tension that had threatened to freeze her limbs.

The wedding coordinator pulled open the double doors again.

At the threshold Daisy stood on the arm of her brother, feeling like a shimmering angel in white, her fingertip veil falling gently from a crown of roses.

The aisle seemed so long, Jack so far away, surrounded at the altar by the crowd of loving and supportive friends.

Daisy clutched the small white Bible that Rebecca had carried in her wedding and clung to her brother's arm as they stepped out onto the white satin, petal-strewn carpet.

"Dearly beloved, we are gathered together in the sight of God and these witnesses to join this man and this woman in holy matrimony. . . .

"Who gives this woman to be this man's wife?"

The same words had been repeated for generations, but as Daisy looked up into Jack's loving brown eyes, she felt as if they had been written just for them.

The promises, for richer for poorer, in sickness and in health—whatever the future held—with Jack by her side, there would always be hope and love and joy.

Now and forever.

A Letter To Our Readers

Dear Reader:

In order that we might better contribute to your reading enjoyment, we would appreciate your taking a few minutes to respond to the following questions. We welcome your comments and read each form and letter we receive. When completed, please return to the following:

Fiction Editor
Heartsong Presents
PO Box 719
Uhrichsville, Ohio 44683

1. Did you enjoy reading *He Loves Me, He Loves Me Not* by Rachel Druten?
   ❏ Very much! I would like to see more books by this author!
   ❏ Moderately. I would have enjoyed it more if

   _____

   _____

   _____

2. Are you a member of **Heartsong Presents**? ❏ Yes ❏ No
   If no, where did you purchase this book? _____

   _____

3. How would you rate, on a scale from 1 (poor) to 5 (superior), the cover design? _____

4. On a scale from 1 (poor) to 10 (superior), please rate the following elements.

   ____ Heroine   ____ Plot
   ____ Hero   ____ Inspirational theme
   ____ Setting   ____ Secondary characters

5. These characters were special because?_____

_____

_____

6. How has this book inspired your life?_____

_____

_____

7. What settings would you like to see covered in future
   Heartsong Presents books? _____

_____

_____

8. What are some inspirational themes you would like to see
   treated in future books? _____

_____

_____

9. Would you be interested in reading other **Heartsong
   Presents** titles?   ❑ Yes   ❑ No

10. Please check your age range:
   ❑ Under 18   ❑ 18-24
   ❑ 25-34   ❑ 35-45
   ❑ 46-55   ❑ Over 55

Name_____

Occupation _____

Address _____

City_____ State_____ Zip_____

COLORADO

4 stories in 1

Taming the frontier is a daunting task—one that can't be burdened by the luxuries of life, including romance. Four settlers take the challenge and are surprised when love springs up beside them along the way.

Four complete inspirational romance stories by author Rosey Dow.

Historical, paperback, 464 pages, 5 ³/₁₆" x 8"

♥ ♥ ♥ ♥ ♥ ♥ ♥ ♥ ♥ ❤ ♥ ♥ ♥ ♥ ♥ ♥ ♥ ♥ ♥

♥ ♥ ♥ ♥ ♥ ♥ ♥ ♥ ♥ ❤ ♥ ♥ ♥ ♥ ♥ ♥ ♥ ♥ ♥

Heartsong

Presents

Great Inspirational Romance at a Great Price!

Heartsong Presents books are inspirational romances in contemporary and historical settings, designed to give you an enjoyable, spirit-lifting reading experience. You can choose wonderfully written titles from some of today's best authors like Peggy Darty, Sally Laity, Tracie Peterson, Colleen L. Reece, Debra White Smith, and many others.

When ordering quantities less than twelve, above titles are $2.97 each.
Not all titles may be available at time of order.

_H_EARTSONG ♥ PRESENTS

Love Stories Are Rated G!

That's for godly, gratifying, and of course, great! If you love a thrilling love story but don't appreciate the sordidness of some popular paperback romances, **Heartsong Presents** is for you. In fact, **Heartsong Presents** is the premiere inspirational romance book club featuring love stories where Christian faith is the primary ingredient in a marriage relationship.

Sign up today to receive your first set of four, never-before-published Christian romances. Send no money now; you will receive a bill with the first shipment. You may cancel at any time without obligation, and if you aren't completely satisfied with any selection, you may return the books for an immediate refund!

Imagine. . .four new romances every four weeks—two historical, two contemporary—with men and women like you who long to meet the one God has chosen as the love of their lives. . .all for the low price of $10.99 postpaid.

To join, simply complete the coupon below and mail to the address provided. **Heartsong Presents** romances are rated G for another reason: They'll arrive Godspeed!

YES! Sign me up for Hearts♥ng!